Table of Contents

Introduction

The Life and Strange Adventures of

Robinson Crusoe

by

Daniel Defoe

CORE CLASSICS®

SERIES EDITOR MICHAEL J. MARSHALL

EDITED AND ABRIDGED BY MICHAEL J. MARSHALL

LIBRARY OF CONGRESS CATALOG CARD NUMBER: 97-75282

ISBN 978-1-890517-02-1 TRADE PAPERBACK

COPYRIGHT © 2001 CORE KNOWLEDGE FOUNDATION

ALL RIGHTS RESERVED · PRINTED IN CANADA

SIXTH PRINTING

DESIGNED BY BILL WOMACK INCORPORATED

COVER ILLUSTRATION BY GB McINTOSH

TEXT ILLUSTRATIONS BY LOUIS AND FREDERICK RHEAD

CORE KNOWLEDGE FOUNDATION

801 EAST HIGH STREET

CHARLOTTESVILLE, VIRGINIA 22902

www.coreknowledge.org

Introduction

THE STORY OF ROBINSON CRUSOE was inspired by a real-life castaway. In 1705, Alexander Selkirk, a Scotsman, argued angrily with the captain of his ship over whether their boat was too leaky to sail. After the boat stopped to get fresh water at an island in the Pacific Ocean, Selkirk refused to go back on board. So the captain left him there alone with a Bible, a gun, a kettle, and a few tools and supplies. Four-and-a-half years later another English ship visiting the island saw a signal fire and found Selkirk still alive. Today, the island is named for him.

Selkirk lived off goat meat and what he called "cabbages that grow on trees." He slept in a hut made of branches and wore goatskin clothes, though for a while he went naked. He was very fit and could catch goats to eat even though he was running barefoot. The sailors who found him said he looked wild. He had mostly forgotten how to speak and at first could say only parts of words.

Selkirk came home to England and Daniel Defoe read about him in newspapers. Selkirk's adventure had Defoe's favorite story ingredients: danger, escape, and survival – plus an ordinary person for its hero. Many more merchants and workers were learning to read and write around the time Defoe wrote *Robinson Crusoe*. To appeal to these new readers, Defoe presented his story as if it was told by an ordinary man who had been rescued from a desert island. He also wrote it in a plain, informative style with a lot of realistic details. This made it easier for many readers to feel they understood Crusoe. One reason *Robinson Crusoe* is still well-liked is that Defoe makes ordinary things seem beautiful and ordinary actions seem noble.

Besides travel adventures, books about personal religious experiences were also very popular in Defoe's day. *Robinson Crusoe* is also like those. Defoe's story tells how Crusoe disobeyed his father by running away to sea, how he survived a shipwreck on a wild island, and how he must work and wait alone, hoping for rescue. Defoe's readers would have seen the similarity to the Biblical story of how Adam and Eve disobeyed God by eating forbidden fruit, how they were thrown out of the Garden of Eden as punishment, and made to work and suffer in hopes that one day they would be forgiven and saved.

In our world of television and radio we seldom have to feel all alone or live in silence. This makes Robinson Crusoe's story thrilling for us. Could you civilize a wilderness like he did, or would it turn you wild, as it did Alexander Selkirk?

E.D. Hirsch Jr.
Charlottesville, Virginia

The Life
and
Strange
Adventures
of

*Robinson
Crusoe*

CHAPTER 1

The First Voyage

I WAS BORN IN THE YEAR 1632, in the city of York, of a good family. My father was a foreigner from **Bremen**, who got a good fortune as a merchant and, leaving off his trade, lived afterwards at York. There he married my mother, whose relations were named Robinson. For them I was called Robinson Kreutznaer, but our

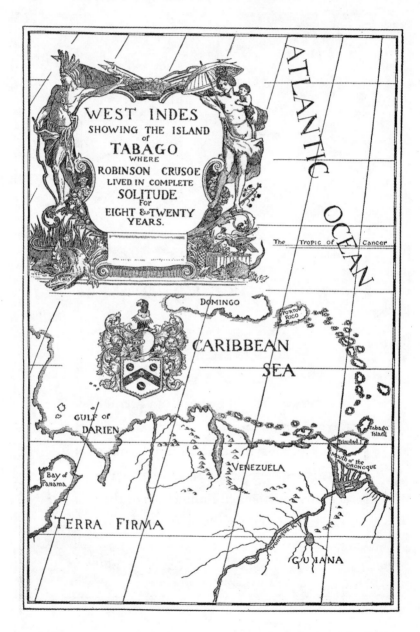

WEST INDES
SHOWING THE ISLAND
of
TABAGO
WHERE
ROBINSON CRUSOE
LIVED IN COMPLETE
SOLITUDE
For
EIGHT & TWENTY
YEARS.

ATLANTIC OCEAN

The   Tropic of   Cancer

DOMINGO

PORTO
RICO

CARIBBEAN
SEA

GULF of
DARIEN

Bay of
Panama

VENEZUELA

Tabago
Island

Trinidad

Mouth of the
ORONOQUE

TERRA FIRMA

Oronoque R.

GUIANA

neighbors pronounced our name Crusoe, **BREMEN** **A port city on the North Sea coast of Germany.** and so my companions have always called me.

I had two elder brothers. One was killed in battle against the Spaniards. What became of my second brother I never knew, just as my father and mother never knew what became of me.

Being the third son, my head was filled early with rambling thoughts. My father, who was very ancient, intended me to be a lawyer, but I was satisfied with nothing but going to sea. My inclination to this led me strongly against the commands of my father and against all the pleas of my mother and friends. There seemed to be something in my nature that led me directly into a life of misery.

My father, a wise man, gave me excellent advice. He called me one morning into his room and asked me what reasons I had for leaving my home and country, where I had the prospect of raising my fortune and living a life of ease and pleasure. He told me that mine was the middle station in life, which he had found by long experience was the best suited to happiness. This was the state that other people envied, between the low and the

MY FATHER, A WISE MAN, GAVE ME EXCELLENT ADVICE.

high, and that a wise man had said as much when he prayed to have neither **poverty nor riches**.

He said I would always find that the calamities of life are not shared among all men. Temperance, moderation, quietness, and health are the blessings of the middle way. This way men went smoothly and gently through the world, not sold as slaves for daily bread, or enraged by passions of envy or ambition. He urged me very affectionately not to throw myself into miseries I need not suffer.

I was sincerely affected by this talk and resolved to settle at home as my

POVERTY NOR RICHES
One of the proverbs of Solomon in the Bible (Old Testament: Proverbs 30:8).

father desired. But in a few days it all wore off, and to prevent my father from influencing me, I decided to run away. However, I did not act hastily. I took my mother aside and told her I was determined to see the world, but if she would speak to my father to let me go on one voyage, and I came back and did not like it, I would promise to go no more.

This put my mother in a great passion. She said it would do no good to speak to my father because he would not consent to anything that would hurt me. In short, if I meant to ruin myself, there was no help for me. She reported this to my father, who said with a sigh, "That boy might be happy if he stays home, but if he goes abroad he will be the most miserable wretch that ever was born."

It was not until almost a year later that I broke loose, though in the meantime I continued to argue with my mother and father about their being so against what I wanted to do. One day in Hull, one of my companions who was going to London by sea in his father's ship urged me to go with him. I asked neither my father nor mother, nor even sent them word of it, but left them to hear of it as they might.

Thus on the first of September, 1651, I went aboard a ship, and never, I believe, did any young adventurer's misfortunes begin sooner or last longer than mine. The ship was no sooner out of the river than the wind began to blow and the waves to rise. As I had never been to sea before, I was most sick in body and terrified in my mind. I began to reflect on what I had done and how justly I was treated by heaven for my wicked leaving of my father and abandoning my duty. My conscience reproached me.

The storm increased and I expected every wave would swallow us up. In this agony of mind I made many vows. If it pleased God to spare my life, if ever I got my foot on dry land again, I would go directly home to my father like a true repenting **prodigal**.

PRODIGAL
A parable of Jesus about a young man who repents of his wasteful, selfish behavior and returns to his father, who gives him a joyous welcome (New Testament: Luke 15:11-32).

These sober thoughts remained while the storm continued. But the next day the wind and sea were calmer. A fine evening followed. The sun went down perfectly clear and rose so the next morning, and the smooth sea

with the sun shining on it was, I thought, the most delight-
ful sight that I ever saw.

I had slept well and was no longer seasick. And
now my companion came to me.

"Well, Bob," said he, clapping me on the shoulder, "I'll wager you were frightened last night when it
blew but a cap full of wind."

"A cap full?" said I. "It was a terrible storm."

"You fool," replied he. "Do you call that a storm?
Why it was nothing at all. We think nothing of a squall
as that. Let's make a bowl of punch and forget all that."

To make short this part of my story, the punch
was made. I was made drunk on it. And in one night's
wickedness I drowned all my repentance and I entirely
forgot all the promises that I made in my distress.
Serious thoughts did return sometimes, but I shook
them off and applied myself to drink and company. I got
as complete a victory over my conscience as any young
fellow could desire.

On the sixth day, we came into Yarmouth Roads
and lay at anchor seven days waiting for a wind that
would take us up the river. But on the eighth day it blew a
terrible storm. I began to see terror and amazement on

the faces even of the seamen. When the master himself came by me and said we shall all be lost, I was dreadfully frightened. The sea went mountains high and washed over us every three or four minutes.

In the middle of the night, one of the men cried out that we had sprung a leak, and there was four feet of water in the hold. All hands were called to the pump. I went and worked very heartily. But the water increased in the hold and it was apparent the ship would sink.

The master continued firing guns to bring help and a ship nearby ventured a boat out to us. It was with the greatest danger that the boat came near. Our men cast them a rope, hauled them close under our stern and we got all into their boat. It was no use to try to reach their ship, so we agreed to pull toward shore.

We were not much more than a quarter-hour off our ship when she sank. I hardly had eyes to look up when the seamen told me she was sinking. From the moment I went in the boat, it was as if my heart was dead within me, partly from fright, partly with horror of what was yet before me.

We could see a great many people running along the shore to assist us when we got near, but we made a slow way. We got in, though not without difficulty, and walked to Yarmouth, where we were treated with great humanity.

Had I had the sense to go back home, I would have been happy, and my father would have even killed the **fatted calf** for me; for hearing that the ship I went away in was cast away at Yarmouth, it was a great while before he learned that I was not drowned.

FATTED CALF
A feast the father prepares to celebrate the return of the prodigal son.

But my ill fate pushed me on. I had several loud calls from my reason to go home, yet I had not the power to do it. I do not know what to call this secret decree that hurries us on to be the causes of our own destruction. Even though we see it, we rush on to it with our eyes open.

My companion, who helped to harden me before, and who was the master's son, was now looking very melancholy. He told his father how I had come on this voyage only for a trial. His father, turning to me in a grave tone, said, "Young man, you ought never to go to sea anymore. You ought to take this for a plain and visible sign that you are not to be a seafarer."

"Why, sir," I said, "will you go to sea no more?"

"It is my calling," said he, "and therefore my

duty. But you have made this voyage for a trial. You see what taste heaven has given you of what you are to expect if you go on. Perhaps this is all befallen us on your account, like **Jonah**. On what account did you go to sea?"

I told him some of my story, at the end of which he burst out with a strange kind of passion. "Young man, depend on it," said he, "if you do not go back, wherever you go, you will meet nothing but disasters and disappoint-ments until your father's words are ful-filled."

JONAH
A prophet of the Old Testament who tried to run away from God and ended up swallowed by a whale, who spit him out after three days.

We parted soon, for I made him little answer. Having some money in my pocket, I travelled to London. As to going home, it occurred to me I would be laughed at by my neighbors and ashamed to see my mother and father. I have since often noticed that the temper of men makes them not ashamed to do what will make them called fools, but ashamed to do what will make them consid-ered wise.

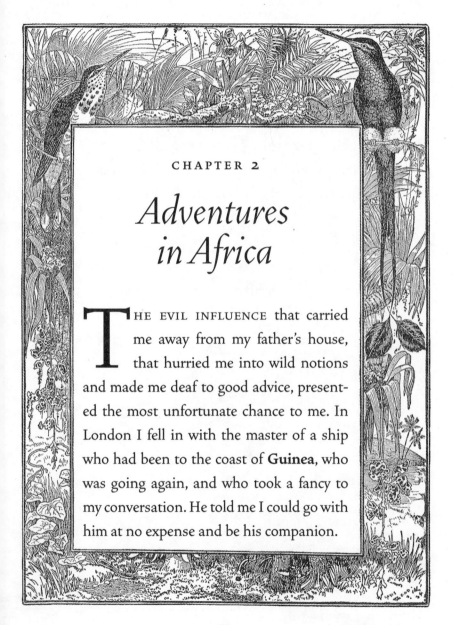

CHAPTER 2

Adventures in Africa

THE EVIL INFLUENCE that carried me away from my father's house, that hurried me into wild notions and made me deaf to good advice, presented the most unfortunate chance to me. In London I fell in with the master of a ship who had been to the coast of **Guinea**, who was going again, and who took a fancy to my conversation. He told me I could go with him at no expense and be his companion.

I entered into friendship with this captain, who was an honest and plain-dealing man. Of all my adventures, this is the only voyage that I may say was successful, which I owe to the integrity of my friend. Under him I also got to know the rules of navigation and to understand some things needful to sailors. This voyage made me both a sailor and a merchant, for I brought home six ounces of gold dust, which filled me with the thoughts that led to my ruin.

I was now set up as a trader. My friend, to my misfortune, died soon after our return. I resolved to make the same voyage again and embarked in the same vessel with his mate, who now had command of the ship. This was the unhappiest voyage a man ever made. Making her course toward the **Canary Islands**, our ship was surprised by a Turkish pirate. We

Canary Islands
Sallee
MOROCCO
Cape Verde
AFRICA
GUINEA

GUINEA
A country on the west coast of Africa.

CANARY ISLANDS
A group of Spanish islands off the northwest coast of Africa that served as a jumping-off point for voyages to the Americas because of favorable ocean currents.

CAPE VERDE
Islands off the west coast of Africa, once part of Portugal.

prepared to fight. About three in the afternoon, he came up with us and we poured a **broadside** in him, which made him sheer off. He attacked us again, this time getting sixty men on our deck, who immediately began hacking the **rigging**. We cleared our deck of them twice. However, with our ship disabled, three of our men killed, and eight wounded, we were forced to give in. They carried us all as prisoners to **Sallee**.

BROADSIDE
A volley of cannonfire from one side of a ship.

RIGGING
The ropes that support the mast and work the sails.

I was kept by the pirate captain and made his slave. I was overwhelmed by this change from merchant to miserable slave. I looked back on my father's prophesy and thought it had come to pass. But, alas, this was but a taste of the misery I was to go through.

I hoped my new master would take me to sea with him, where he might be taken by a Spanish **Man-of-War** and I would be set free. But he left me on shore to look after his garden and do chores around his house. When he was home, he had me stay in his ship's cabin to look after it.

MAN-OF-WAR
A warship.

I thought about nothing but escape. For two years, I never had the least chance, but then an odd circumstance happened. My master, if the weather was fair, would take a small boat out fishing and take me and a young sailor with him. I was very good at catching fish. One time, a fog rose so thick we lost sight of shore. We rowed all night and when morning came we found we had pulled off to sea, instead of toward land. We were at least two **leagues** from shore. We got in again, but we were all very hungry.

LEAGUE
An old unit of distance that represented between two-and-a-half and four miles.

My master was warned by this disaster and resolved to take more care in the future. He ordered his ship's carpenter, who was also an English slave, to build a little cabin in the middle of the long boat he had taken from our ship. It lay very low and snug and had room for him and a slave or two, with some small lockers to keep bread and liquors in.

It happened that he arranged to go out fishing and bird hunting with two or three prominent men of that place and so sent on board the boat a larger store of provisions than usual, including three muskets. I got all the things ready as he directed and waited. By and by, my master came aboard alone and told me his guests had put off going, having some other business. He ordered me, and his man and boy, as usual, to go out and catch him fish, for his friends were to eat at his house that evening.

At that moment notions of deliverance darted into my thoughts, for I was to have the little ship at my command. I prepared, not for fishing, but for a voyage, though I knew not which way I should steer.

After we had fished for a time and caught nothing, I said, "This will not do. Our master is not served thus. We must go farther out to sea." The **Moor**, thinking no harm, agreed, and I ran the boat out to sea a league farther. Giving the boy the tiller, I stepped forward to where the Moor was, acting as if I was getting something behind him. I took him by surprise and tossed him clear overboard. He rose immediately, for he could swim like a cork, and begged to be taken back in. He told me he would go all over the world with me, and he swam so strongly after the boat that I fetched a musket and aimed it at him. I told him I had done him no harm and would do none, if he was quiet.

MOOR
One of a Moslem people living in northern Africa.

"You swim well enough to reach the shore," I said, "and the sea is calm. Make your way to shore, and I will do you no harm, but if you come near the boat I will shoot you through the head, for I am determined to have my liberty." So he turned and swam for shore, and I have no doubt he reached it, for he was an excellent swimmer.

I turned to the boy, whom they called Xury, and said to him, "Xury, if you will be faithful to me, I will make you a great man. But if you do not swear by **Mahomet** to be true to me, I must throw you in the sea, too." The boy smiled and spoke so innocently, that I could not mistrust him. He swore to be faithful to me and go all over the world with me.

MAHOMET The Islamic name for God (now spelled Muhammad).

I steered out to sea, so that the Moors might think I had gone to Gibraltar, as anyone in their wits might be supposed to do. But as it grew dusk, I changed course and steered directly south, bending a little back toward shore. I had such a dreadful fear of falling into the hands of the Moors that I would not stop, or go ashore, or anchor, until I had sailed for five days. My hope was that if I stayed along this shore until I came to the part where the English traded, I could find a vessel that would take us in.

We made on southward, living very sparingly on

"IF YOU COME NEAR THE BOAT
I WILL SHOOT YOU THROUGH THE HEAD."

our provisions, which began to run low, and going
ashore only when we needed fresh water. After about ten
days, I began to see that the land was inhabited. In two
or three places as we sailed by, we saw people stand on
the shore to look at us. We could see they were black and
stark naked.

I once wanted to go to them, but Xury said, "No
go, no go." However, I sailed nearer the shore so I might

talk to them and I found they ran along the shore by me. I kept at a distance but talked to them with signs as well as I could. I particularly made signs for something to eat. They beckoned to me to stop, and I lowered my sail. In a half an hour, they brought some corn and dried meat to the shore and laid it down. They went and stood a great way off until we had fetched it on board our boat, and then they came close again.

We made signs of thanks but had nothing to offer in return. At that very instant, two mighty creatures came with great fury from the mountains. In terrible fright, the people fled. However, the creatures plunged themselves into the sea and swam about as if they came to play. At last, one of them came near the boat and I shot him directly in the head. Immediately he sank, but he rose again and began swimming for shore, struggling for life. Between the wound and the strangling of the water, he died just before he reached shore.

It is impossible to express the astonishment of these poor creatures at the noise and fire of my gun. Some of them were ready to die from fear and fell down in terror. But when they saw the creature dead in the water, they took heart and began searching the shore for it. I found him by the blood stain in the water. It was a leopard, spotted and fine looking. The people held up their hands in admiration to think how I killed him.

The other creature ran directly to the mountains. I made signs to them that they might have the flesh, but made signs also that I wished for the skin, which they gave to me and brought me more food and water as well.

Now furnished with roots and corn, I made forward for eleven days without going near the shore. At length I saw a point of land, which I concluded was **Cape Verde**. All of a sudden, Xury called out, "Master, a ship with a sail!" I saw she was a Portuguese ship on a course out to sea. Using all the sail I had, I found they would be gone by before I could get near enough to signal. But it seems they saw me and shortened sail to let me come up.

CAPE VERDE
See map on page 12.

They asked me what I was in Portuguese, Spanish, and French, but I understood none of them. At last, a Scot who was on board called to me and I told him that I was an Englishman escaped out of slavery from the Moors. Then they very kindly took me in.

I immediately offered all I had to the captain for

saving me. But he generously told me he would take nothing.

"I have saved your life on the terms I would be glad to be saved myself," said he. "I carry you to Brazil, so far away from your own country that if I take what you have, you will starve there. Then I only take away the life I saved."

He offered me sixty pieces of gold for Xury, but I was very reluctant to sell the poor boy's liberty. He had helped me so faithfully to get my own. The captain said he would give the boy a written contract to set him free in ten years, if he turned Christian. Upon Xury saying he was willing to go to him, I let the captain have him.

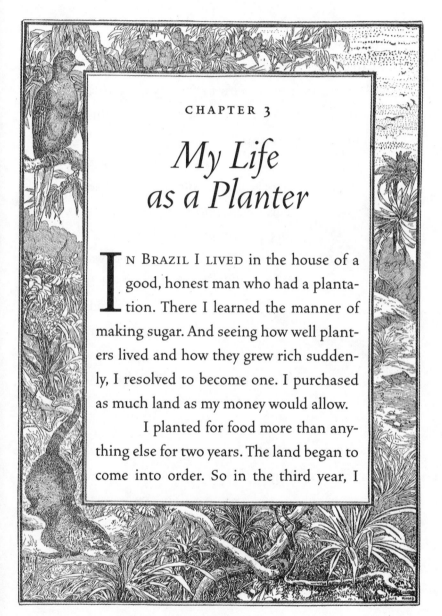

CHAPTER 3

My Life as a Planter

IN BRAZIL I LIVED in the house of a good, honest man who had a plantation. There I learned the manner of making sugar. And seeing how well planters lived and how they grew rich suddenly, I resolved to become one. I purchased as much land as my money would allow.

I planted for food more than anything else for two years. The land began to come into order. So in the third year, I planted some tobacco and made ready to plant sugar cane in the year to come. I wanted help and found I had done wrong in parting with my boy, Xury. But, alas, for me to do wrong was no great wonder. I bought a slave and a **bond servant** also.

BOND SERVANT
Someone who agreed to work for a certain term of years without wages in exhange for passage to the New World.

I went on the next year with great success. I raised fifty rolls of tobacco, well cured. And now increasing in wealth, my head began to be full of projects beyond my reach. Had I continued as I was, I had room for all the happy things my father earnestly recommended. But I could not be content with the view I had of being a rich man on my plantation, but pursued my rash desires of rising fast and so cast myself down into the deepest gulf of misery that ever a man fell into.

I had now the friendship of my fellow planters, and in our talks I often gave them an account of my voyages to the coast of Guinea and trading with the natives there, and how it easy it was to purchase, for trifles such as beads, toys, scissors, and bits of glass, slaves for service in Brazil. They listened closely, especially to that part about buying slaves.

SEEING HOW WELL PLANTERS LIVED AND HOW THEY GREW RICH
SUDDENLY, I RESOLVED TO BECOME ONE.

One morning three of them came to me and made a secret proposal to fit out a ship to make one voyage to Guinea and bring slaves back to divide among their plantations. I would get an equal share of the slaves if I would manage the trading on the coast.

I told them I would go with all my heart, if they would look after my plantation. And so I hurried on, blindly obeying my fancy rather than my reason. All things being prepared as my partners and I agreed, I went on board at an evil hour, eight years to the day since I left my mother and father, in order to act as a rebel and a fool.

Our ship carried six guns and 14 men, besides the captain, his boy and myself. We had no cargo except such toys as we meant to trade. We passed the equator in about twelve days, when a violent hurricane blew us terribly for twelve days. We could do nothing but let it carry us wherever fate and the fury of the wind directed. I expected every day to be swallowed up by the sea. Nor indeed, did any expect to save his life. One of our men died of tropical fever, and one man and the boy were washed overboard.

When finally we could observe our position, we

found we were near the mouth of the **River Orinoco**. The ship being very leaky, we steered toward Barbados, in the Caribbean islands, hoping to find relief. But shortly a second storm came upon us and carried us away again, westward, out of the way of all commerce and into the danger of being devoured by savages.

Orinoco River

VENEZUELA

SOUTH AMERICA

ORINOCO RIVER
The major river of Venezuela.

As the wind was still blowing very hard, one of our men, early one morning, cried out, "land." We had no sooner looked out in hope of seeing it than the ship struck sand and stopped. At that moment, the sea broke over us so that all should have perished immediately. As we could not hope the ship would hold many minutes without breaking in pieces, the men flung her boat over the side. Getting in her and letting go, all eleven of us committed ourselves to the sea.

Now our case was very dismal. We all saw plainly that the sea was so high that the boat could not live and we were all to be drowned. We worked the oars toward the land with heavy hearts, like men going to their execution, for we all knew as the boat reached shore it would

WE HAD NO SOONER LOOKED OUT IN HOPE OF SEEING LAND
THAN THE SHIP STRUCK SAND AND STOPPED.

be dashed into a thousand pieces. We hoped we might happen into some smooth water, like the mouth of a river, but as we came nearer and nearer to shore, the land looked more frightful than the sea.

After we had rowed for a league, a raging wave, mountain-high, came rolling up from behind us. It took us with such fury that it overturned the boat and separated us from each other. That wave buried me 30 feet deep in the sea and I could feel myself carried with a mighty force and swiftness toward the shore. I held my breath and swam with all my might. I was ready to burst when I found my head and hands shoot above water. Though it was only two seconds' time, it gave me breath and new courage. I was covered again with water for a good while, but I held out. I felt ground with my feet and ran with what strength I could toward shore. But twice more I was lifted by waves and carried.

This last time was near fatal to me, for the sea dashed me against a rock and left me senseless, indeed helpless. The blow beat the breath out of my body and had it returned soon, I would have been strangled in the water, for a wave soon covered me. I held to the rock until the wave washed back. Then I fetched

I HELD TO THE ROCK UNTIL THE WAVE WASHED BACK.

another run and clambered up the cliffs of the shore and sat down in the grass, free from danger.

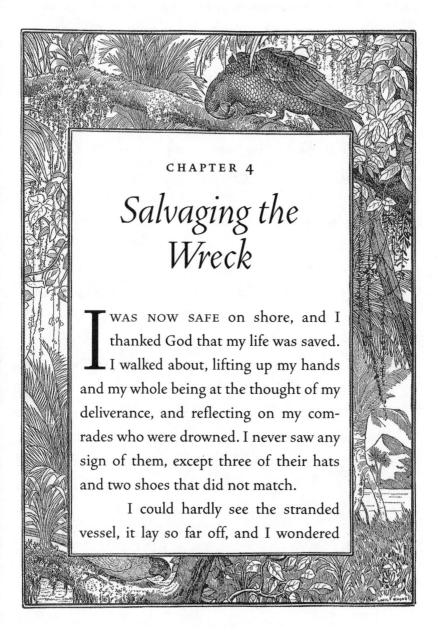

CHAPTER 4

Salvaging the Wreck

I WAS NOW SAFE on shore, and I thanked God that my life was saved. I walked about, lifting up my hands and my whole being at the thought of my deliverance, and reflecting on my comrades who were drowned. I never saw any sign of them, except three of their hats and two shoes that did not match.

I could hardly see the stranded vessel, it lay so far off, and I wondered how I had gotten to shore. I began to look around me to see what was next to do. I had no clothes, nothing to eat or drink, nor any prospect but perishing from hunger. I had no weapon to hunt with or defend myself against other creatures. All I had was a knife, a pipe, and a little tobacco in a box.

With night coming on, I began to consider what would happen to me if any beasts in that country came upon me while searching for prey. The remedy I thought of was to get up in a thick, bushy tree, like a fir, but thorny, and sit all night, thinking what sort of death I might die the next day. I put a little tobacco in my mouth to prevent hunger, cut a short stick for defense, got up in a tree near me, and fell fast asleep. I slept comfortably and found myself refreshed.

When I awoke, the weather was clear. I was surprised to see that in the night the ship was lifted by the swelling of the tide and driven almost as far as the rock on which I had been so bruised. This being within a mile of the shore, I wished I might save some things from it for my use. I found the boat, which the sea had tossed up on land about two miles down the shore. I walked as far as I could to get to her, but found a broad inlet of water between me and the boat, so I came back, being more intent upon getting at the ship, where I hoped to find food.

After noon, the tide ebbed so far out that I could come within a quarter-mile of the ship. Here I found a fresh grief, for I saw that if we all had kept on board, we would have all gotten safely to shore, and I would not be so miserably alone. This forced tears from my eyes again.

I pulled off my clothes, for the weather was extremely hot, and took to the water. But when I came to the ship, my difficulty was to know how to get on board, for she lay aground high out of the water. I swam around twice, and the second time I spied a small piece of rope hanging down low. With great difficulty I got hold of it, and by that help I got up into the **forecastle** of the ship. I found that the ship was **staved in** and had a great deal of water in her hold.

FORECASTLE
The front part of a ship, where sailors usually slept.

STAVED IN
Crushed or smashed inward.

My first work was to see what was spoiled, and I found that all the ship's provisions were dry and untouched by the water. Being very hungry, I filled my pockets with biscuits and ate them as

AFTER THROWING AS MANY PIECES OF WOOD OVERBOARD
AS I COULD, I WENT DOWN THE SHIP'S SIDE.

I went about other things, for I had no time to lose. Now I wanted nothing but a boat to furnish myself with many things that would be very necessary to me.

It was in vain to sit and wish for what was not to be had. We had several spare **yards** and two or three large spars of wood, and a spare topmast. I fell to work with these and flung as many of them overboard as I could manage for their weight, tying every one with a rope so that they might not drift away. When this was done I went down the ship's side and tied four of them fast together at both ends, as well as I could, in the form of a raft. I found I could walk on it very well, but it was not able to bear any great weight. So I went to work and cut a spare topmast into three lengths and added them to my raft.

My next care was what to load it with and how to preserve what I laid upon it from the surf. I first laid all the boards upon it I could get, and having considered well what I most wanted, I got three seamen's chests, which I broke open and emptied, and lowered them down on the raft. The first I filled with food: bread, rice, cheese, dried goat flesh, and a little corn we had laid by

YARDS
Tapered wooden poles, at right angles to the mast, that hold up sails.

to feed the fowl we brought to sea with us. I found several cases of bottles belonging to our skipper, which contained **cordial waters**, which I stowed by themselves. While doing this I found the tide began to flow and saw my coat and shirt, which I had left on the sand, float away. This put me rummaging for clothes, of which I found enough, but I had other things my eye was more upon. After long searching, I found the carpenter's chest, which was more valuable to me than a shipload of gold would have been at that time.

CORDIAL WATERS
Liqueurs, such as brandy; usually sweetened alcoholic drinks flavored with nuts, fruit, or spices.

My next care was for some ammunition and arms. There were two very good **fowling pieces** in the cabin and two pistols, some powder horns, and two rusty old swords. These I took. With much searching, I found three barrels of gunpowder, two of them still dry, which I got to my raft.

FOWLING PIECE
A shotgun.

Now I began to think how I could get to shore, having neither sail nor oar. The sea was smooth and calm. The tide was rising and what little wind there was blew toward land. Besides the tools in the chest, I found two saws, an axe, and a hammer, and

I FOUND A STRONG CURRENT, SO I GUIDED MY RAFT AS WELL AS
I COULD. BUT HERE I ALMOST SUFFERED A SECOND SHIPWRECK.

three broken oars, and with this cargo, I put to sea.

For about a mile my raft did very well, though I drifted a little from the place where I landed before. There appeared before me a little opening of land, and I found a strong current into it, so I guided my raft as well as I could. But here I almost suffered a second shipwreck. If I had, I think it would have broken my heart. Knowing nothing of the coast, I ran one end of my raft aground on a **shoal**. All my cargo slipped towards the end that was still afloat. I did my utmost by setting my back against the chests to keep them in their places. I dared not stir from the posture I was in, holding up the chests with all my might. I stood in that manner more than half an hour until the rising tide floated my raft again. I pushed her off with the oar and at length I found myself in a little river with land on both sides.

SHOAL
A sandbar that makes the water very shallow.

I was not willing to go too far up the river. Hoping in time to see some ship at sea, I wished to stay as near the coast as I could. I spied a little cove on the right side of the creek, to which I guided my raft with great difficulty. The shore being pretty steep, there was no place to land that would not have dipped my cargo in the sea. All that I could do was keep the raft near a flat piece of ground. I fastened her there by sticking my two broken oars in the ground on either side of her, and thus I waited until the water ebbed away and left my raft and cargo safe on shore.

My next work was to view the country and seek a place for my dwelling, and a place to stow my goods to secure them from whatever might happen. I yet knew not whether I was on a continent or an island, whether it was inhabited or uninhabited, and whether I was in danger from wild beasts or not. There was a hill a mile from me, which rose very steep and high, and which seemed higher than some other hills that lay in a ridge from it northward. I took one of the fowling pieces, one of the pistols, and a horn of powder, and traveled for discovery to the top of that hill. There I saw my fate. I was on an island. No land could be seen, except some rocks a great way off, and two smaller islands about three leagues to the west.

I found also that the island was barren and uninhabited, except by wild beasts. I saw an abundance of fowl, but did not know their kind. Coming back, I shot at a great bird I saw sitting in a tree. I believe it was the first gun ever fired there since the creation of the world. I had no sooner fired, than from all parts of the woods there arose countless fowl of many sorts, making a confused screaming. As for the creature I killed, I took it to be a kind of hawk, but it had no talons and it was not fit to eat.

I came back to my raft and fell to work to bring my cargo on shore, which took me the rest of the day. I knew not what to do with myself at night, for I was afraid to lie down on the ground where some wild beast might devour me, though I afterwards found there was really no need for those fears.

I barricaded myself around with the chests and boards I had and made a kind of hut. As for food, I yet saw no way to supply myself, except that I had seen two creatures like rabbits run out of the woods where I shot the fowl.

I began to consider that I might get a great many useful things out of the ship, particularly ropes and sails, and I decided to make another voyage to the vessel. I knew the first storm must break her all in pieces. I resolved to set all other things aside until I got everything out of the ship that I could get. I went as before,

I CAME BACK TO MY RAFT AND FELL TO WORK TO BRING MY
CARGO ON SHORE, WHICH TOOK ME THE REST OF THE DAY.

only I stripped down before I left my hut.

I got on board in the same way and prepared a second raft. I brought away from the carpenter's stores three bags full of nails and spikes, a great screwjack, a dozen hatchets, and the most useful thing, a grindstone. From the gunner's things, I took three iron crowbars, two barrels of musket bullets, seven muskets, another fowling piece, more gunpowder, and a large bag full of small shot. I took all the clothes I could find, a spare topsail, a hammock, and some bedding. All this I loaded on my raft and brought safely on shore to my very great comfort.

I was afraid while I was absent that my provisions on shore might be devoured, but when I came back, I found no sign of any visitor, except a creature like a cat that sat on one of the chests. When I came toward it, it ran away a little distance and stood still. She sat very composed and looked into my face, as if she had a mind to get acquainted. I pointed my gun at her, but she did not understand it and did not move away. I tossed her a bit of biscuit, though my supply was not great. However, I did spare her a bit, as I say, and she went to it, smelled it and ate it and looked for more. But I could spare no more, so she marched off.

I went to work to make a little tent with the sail and some poles. I brought everything inside that I thought would spoil from either sun or rain, and I piled the empty chests and casks in a circle around the tent to fortify it. I blocked up the door with some boards and stood a chest on end. Spreading one of the beds on the ground and laying my pistols and a gun beside me, I went to bed for the first time and slept very quietly all night, for I was very weary.

Every day at low water I went on board and brought away something or other. I brought away all the small ropes and all the sails, only I had to cut them in pieces and they were useful merely as canvas.

But what comforted me more was, after six such voyages, I found a **hogshead** of bread and three casks of rum, a box of sugar, and a barrel of fine flour. This surprised me because I had given up expecting to find any more food. I wrapped up the bread in pieces of sails and got all this on shore safely also.

I had now been on shore 13 days and brought away all that one pair of hands could bring, though I believe, if the calm weather

HOGSHEAD
A large barrel that holds between 63 and 140 gallons.

had held, I would have brought away the whole ship piece by piece. But on the twelfth time on board, though I had rummaged through the cabin so that I thought nothing more could be found, I did find a locker containing three razors, a pair of scissors, a dozen good knives and forks, and 36 pounds of money, some gold coins and some silver.

I smiled to myself at this sight. "O drug!" I said aloud. "What art thou good for? One of those knives is worth all this heap to me." However, on second thought, I took it away, wrapped in a piece of canvas. While I was preparing this, the wind began to rise and in a quarter of an hour a fresh gale began to blow from shore. It was in vain to make a raft. So I swam across the channel, with great difficulty, partly because of the weight of things I had about me, and partly from the roughness of the water.

I got home to my little tent, where I lay secure with my wealth about me. The storm blew very hard all night, and in the morning when I looked out, no more ship was to be seen. I was surprised, but comforted myself with the thought that I had lost no time, nor spared any effort, to get everything useful out of her.

CHAPTER 5

Building My Home

MY THOUGHTS were now entirely about securing myself against either savages, should any appear, or wild beasts. I had many thoughts of how to do this, whether I should make a cave or a tent, and, in the end, I decided on both.

The place I was in was not good for settlement because it was on marshy ground, which I believed would be unhealthy, and because there was no fresh water near it.

In search of a proper place, I found a little green plain on the side of a hill. Where the hill met the flat green it was as steep as the side of a house, so nothing could come down on me from the top. In the side of this rock was a hollow place, worn away like the door of a cave, though there was not really any way into the rock at all. Just before this hollow place I resolved to pitch my tent. This plain was about a hundred yards wide and twice as long, and at the end descended down to the seaside. It was sheltered from the heat every day until the sun was about to set.

Before I set up the tent, I drew a half circle in front of the hollow place about twenty yards in diameter. In this circle I pitched two rows of strong stakes, driving them into the ground until they stood very firm. The biggest end was out of the ground about six feet and sharpened on the end. I took lengths of chain I had cut from the ship and laid them between the two rows of stakes, which were six inches from each other, up to the top. This fence was so strong that neither man nor beast could get through it or over it. It cost me a great deal of labor.

The entrance was not through a door, but by a short ladder over the top that, when I was in, I lifted over after me, so I was completely fenced in. Into this fortress I carried all my riches, all my food and ammunition, and made me a large tent to keep me from the rains that, in one part of the year, are very violent there.

Now I began to work my way into the rock, laying all the stones I dug within my fence in the nature of a terrace. Thus I made a cave behind my tent that served as a cellar. About this time, in a storm, a flash of lightning happened. I was not so much surprised at the lightning as the thought that darted into my mind as swift as lightning itself: My powder! My heart sank when I thought that at one blast all my powder might be destroyed. Not only my defense, but my food entirely depended on it.

After the storm was over, I applied myself to make bags to separate the powder, in hope that whatever might come, it would not all take fire at once. I kept the parcels apart so that one should not fire another. I made 100 parcels and placed them in my new cave, which I fancied to call my kitchen, and some I hid in holes in the rocks, marking them very carefully.

I went out at least once every day with my gun to see if I could kill anything for food and to acquaint myself with the island. I presently discovered that there were goats on the island. But they were so shy, so subtle, so swift of foot, that it was the most difficult thing in the world to come at them. I was not discouraged, for after I found out their haunts, I laid in wait for them. I observed that their sight was directed downward so that they did not easily see objects above them. Afterwards I always climbed to get above them and then I had a fair mark.

The first shot I had at these creatures, I killed a she-goat. She had a little kid beside her, which grieved me heartily. When the old one fell, the kid stood stock still until I came and took her up. And when I carried the old one on my shoulders, the kid followed me to my enclosure. I carried the kid over the fence, in hopes to raise it up tame, but it would not eat, so I was forced to kill it and eat it myself. These two provided my meat for a great while, for I ate sparingly and saved my food as much as I could.

I had a dismal outlook. I considered it to be the will of Heaven that I should end my life in this desolate place. I called it the Island of Despair. Tears ran down my face when I had these thoughts. Sometimes I would

I CARRIED THE KID OVER THE FENCE, IN HOPES TO RAISE IT UP TAME,
BUT IT WOULD NOT EAT, SO I WAS FORCED TO KILL AND EAT IT MYSELF.

INTO THE POST I CUT THESE WORDS:
I CAME ON SHORE HERE ON THE 30TH OF SEPT. 1659.

wonder why Providence should so ruin his creatures, make them so absolutely miserable, that it could hardly be rational to be thankful for such a life.

But something always checked these thoughts. One day while walking with my gun by the sea, my reason asked me, "Why were you singled out to be saved?" Evils must be considered with the good that is in them. Then it occurred to me again that I was well-supplied for survival. What would I have done without a gun or tools or clothes? I had these, and health.

And now, entering into the story of my melancholy, silent life, such perhaps as was never heard of in the world before, I shall take it from the beginning and continue in order.

After I had been on the island about twelve days, I began to worry I would lose my reckoning of time. To prevent this, I set up a large post on the shore where I first landed, and with my knife cut on it the words: *I came on shore here on the 30th of sept. 1659*. On the sides of this square post I cut a notch every day and every seventh day the notch was twice as long as the rest. Thus I kept my calendar.

I should mention that I brought out of the ship several things of less value but not at all less useful to me. In particular, I secured pens, ink, paper, parcels belonging to the captain, mate and gunner, compasses, spyglasses, charts, Bibles and prayer books, and several other books. And I must not forget the ship's dog and two cats. I carried both cats with me. The dog jumped out of the ship for himself and swam to shore. He was a trusty servant to me for many years. I only wanted him to talk to me, but that he would not do. I had these things, but I lacked others, such as a pick-axe, a shovel, and needles and thread.

I drew up the state of my affairs in writing, not so much to leave them to anyone who would come after me, but to prevent my thoughts from afflicting my mind. There is scarcely any condition in the world so miserable that there is not something to be thankful for in it. As my reason began to master my sadness, I gave up looking out to sea to see if I could spy a ship and applied myself to making things as easy for me as I could.

After some time, I think it was about a year-and-a-half, I raised up a wall of turf, about two feet thick on the outside, against my fence, and I raised rafters from it to the rock. I covered it with the boughs of trees. I also set myself to enlarge my cave to make room to order my goods. The loose, sandy rock yielded

I BEGAN TO MAKE SUCH NECESSARY THINGS AS A TABLE AND A CHAIR.

to my labor. I worked sideways to my right and so worked quite around and made a door to come out on the outside of my fort. This gave me not only a way in and out, but room to stow my goods.

Now I began to make such necessary things as a table and a chair, for without these I was not able to enjoy the few comforts I had. I could not write or eat or do several things with pleasure without a table.

So I went to work. By making the most logical judgments of things, every man may master every mechanical art. I had never handled a tool in my life, yet in time, by labor and effort, I found I could make whatever I wanted, especially if I had tools. I made an abundance of things with no more than an **adze** and a hatchet. If I wanted a board, I had no other way but to cut down a tree, hew it flat on each side with my axe and then smooth it with my adze. By this method I could make only one board out of a whole tree, but my labor was as well-employed this way as another.

ADZE
A short-handled, hoe-like cutting tool used to shape logs into timbers or planks.

However, I made my table and chair out of short boards that I had brought from the ship. I made large shelves along the side of my cave, to separate everything into their places, so that I might easily come at them. It was a great pleasure to see all my goods in such order.

Having settled my household stuff and made all around me as handsome as I could, I began to keep a journal, of which I shall here give you a copy, though not of some things I have already told you. I kept it until I ran out of ink.

THE JOURNAL

December 27

Killed a young goat and lamed another and led it home on a string. I bound up its leg, which was broken. I took care of it and the leg grew as strong as ever. By my nursing it so long, it grew tame and fed on the little green outside my door and would not go away. This was the first time I thought of breeding tame creatures to be my food when my ammunition was all gone.

January 1

Very hot still. This evening, going farther into the center of the island, I found plenty of goats, though shy and hard to come at. I resolved to bring my dog to hunt them.

January 2

I went out with the dog and set him against the goats, but I was mistaken. They all faced about on him. He knew his danger too well and would not come near them.

April 14

I finished my wall with a thickness of turf against it. I persuaded myself that if any people were to come on shore they would not see anything like a dwelling.

I was in great need of a candle. As soon as it was dark, which was generally by seven o'clock, I was forced to go to bed. The only remedy I had was, when I killed a goat, I saved its fat, and in a little dish I made of clay, which I baked in the sun, I placed some **oakum** as a wick and made me a lamp. This gave me light, though not a clear light like a candle.

OAKUM
Loose rope fiber, used for caulking seams in wooden ships.

Rummaging in my things I found a little bag that had held corn to feed our poultry on the ship. I shook the bag out on the outside of my fort. About a month after, or thereabouts, I saw some few stalks of something green shooting out of the ground. I was perfectly astonished when, after a little longer time, I saw ten or twelve ears come out, which were our English barley.

It is impossible to express the confusion of my thoughts on this. The barley startled me strangely, and I suggested to myself that God had miraculously caused this grain to grow, without the help of any seed, to be food for me. This touched my heart. And more strange was that near it were some other straggling stalks, which I knew to be rice because I had seen it grown in Africa. At last it occurred to me that I shook out the bag of chicken feed in that place, and then the wonder began to fade. My thankfulness to God lessened, too, upon the discovery that this was nothing uncommon. But I should have seen that it really was the work of Providence that ten or twelve grains should remain unspoiled after rats ate all the rest, or that I happened to throw it in that place and at that time.

I carefully saved all the grain and resolved to sow it again. I hoped in time to raise enough to supply me with bread. But it was not until the fourth year that I could spare any to eat. I lost all I sowed in the first season by not planting at the proper time.

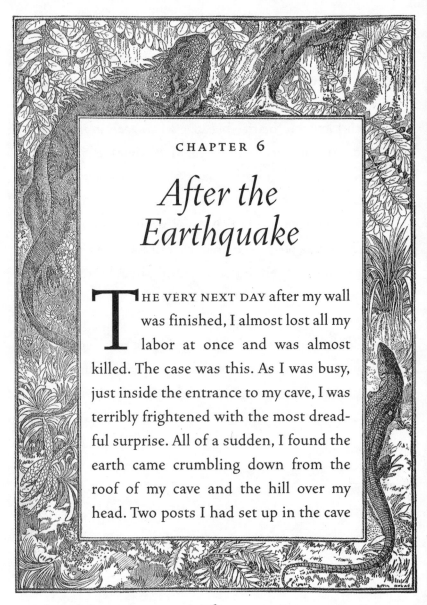

CHAPTER 6

After the Earthquake

THE VERY NEXT DAY after my wall was finished, I almost lost all my labor at once and was almost killed. The case was this. As I was busy, just inside the entrance to my cave, I was terribly frightened with the most dreadful surprise. All of a sudden, I found the earth came crumbling down from the roof of my cave and the hill over my head. Two posts I had set up in the cave cracked in a frightful manner. I was heartily scared. From fear I would be buried inside, I ran to my ladder and got over my wall. I no sooner stepped down on the ground than I felt a terrible earthquake. The ground shook three times, about eight minutes apart, with such shocks as would have overturned the strongest buildings on earth. The sea was put into violent motion, and I believe the shocks were stronger under the water than on the island.

I was so amazed, never having felt anything like it, that I was like one dead. The motion of the earth made my stomach sick like one tossed at sea. But the noise of falling rock awakened me, so to speak. I thought of nothing but the hill falling on my tent and my goods and burying them. This sunk my soul a second time.

After the third shock was over and I felt no more for some time, I began to take courage. I had not heart enough to go over the wall again for fear of being buried alive. I sat on the ground, greatly downcast, not knowing what to do. While I sat, the sky grew cloudy and soon the wind rose, and in half an hour it blew a dreadful hurricane. The sea was covered with foam and froth. The shore was covered with water. Trees were torn up by the roots. This went on for about three hours and then it began to rain very hard.

All this time I sat on the ground very terrified and dejected. Suddenly it came to me that the rain meant the earthquake itself was over. I went in and sat in my tent, but the rain was so violent that my tent was ready to be beaten down with it. I was forced to go into my cave, though I was very much afraid it would fall on my head. I took a small sip of rum to support my spirits, which I always did very sparingly, knowing I could have no more when it was gone.

It continued raining all night and most of the next day, so I could not go out. I began to think of what would be best to do. If the island was subject to earthquakes, there would be no living in a cave for me. I must consider building some little hut in an open place that I might surround with a wall. If I stayed where I was, I would certainly, sometime or another, be buried alive. I spent the next two days thinking of where to move my tent. Still, when I looked about and saw how everything was put in order and how well-concealed I was, how safe from danger, it made me reluctant to move.

I decided that I would go to work with all speed to build a wall of poles and ropes, in a circle, and would set up my tent inside it once it was finished. In the meantime I would stay where I was.

April 22

My three large axes and many hatchets were all full of notches and dull from chopping and cutting knotty, hard wood. I was at a loss about them. I had a grindstone, but I could not turn it and hold the tools too. This cost me as much thought as a statesman over a point of politics or a judge over the life and death of a man. At length I contrived a wheel, with a string to turn it with my foot, that let me have both hands at liberty. I have never seen such a thing in England. It cost me a week's work to bring to perfection.

April 28

I took two days grinding my tools.

AT LENGTH I CONTRIVED A WHEEL, WITH A STRING TO TURN IT
WITH MY FOOT, THAT LET ME HAVE BOTH HANDS AT LIBERTY.

April 30

Seeing my bread is low, I reduced myself to one biscuit a day.

May 1

In the morning, looking toward the sea, I saw something lying on the shore bigger than ordinary. It looked like a cask. When I came to it, I found a small barrel and two or three other pieces of the wreck of the ship, which were driven on shore by the hurricane. The wreck itself seemed higher out of the water. The barrel was full of gunpowder, but it had gotten wet and was caked as hard as stone. I rolled it farther up on shore, and went on as near as I could to the wreck.

When I came to the ship, I found it had moved. I could now walk up to her when the tide was out. This entirely changed my plans from moving my dwelling. I busied myself mightily to make my way inside the ship, but it was choked up with sand. I resolved to pull everything to pieces that I could, believing everything would be of some use or other to me.

May 3

I cut a beam through, but as the tide came in I was forced to stop.

May 4

I went fishing, but caught not one fish I could eat. I had no hooks, yet I frequently caught fish. I dried them in the sun and ate them dry.

May 5

Worked on the wreck. Cut another beam and brought three planks off the deck.

May 6

Worked on the wreck. Got several iron bolts and other pieces of iron work. Came home very tired.

May 24

Every day to this day I worked on the

wreck. I loosened some things so much with the crowbar that with the first strong tide several casks and two seamen's chests floated out, but did not come to shore.

June 16

Going down to the sea, I found a large turtle, the first I had ever seen. Had I happened to be on the other side of the island, I found out later, I would have seen hundreds every day.

June 17

I cooked the turtle and found 60 eggs in her. Her meat was to me at that time the best I had ever tasted in my life.

June 18

Rained all day and I stayed in. I was chilly, which I knew was not usual.

June 19

Very ill and shivering.

June 20

Violent pain in my head and fever.

June 21

Very ill. Frightened to death to be so sick. Prayed to God.

June 25

Shivering fit so violent it held me for seven hours. Cold and hot fits. Faint sweats.

June 26

Better, but very weak. Killed a goat and broiled some of it. I would have preferred to stew it, but I have no pot.

June 27

Shivering fit again so violent that I lay in bed all day. I was ready to perish from thirst. I had no strength to stand up. In the morning, I had this terrible dream:

I thought I was sitting outside my wall on the ground, where I sat in the storm, and

that I saw a man come down from a black
cloud, in a bright flame of fire. He was all
over as bright as flame, and I could just
bear to look at him. His face was dreadful.
When he stepped on the ground with his
feet, I thought the earth trembled, just as
it had in the earthquake.

He moved toward me with a long spear to
kill me. As he came near, he spoke to me
in a voice so terrible it is impossible to
express. All I understood was this:
"Seeing all these things have not brought
you to repentance, now you shall die." At
these words, I thought he lifted up the
spear to kill me.

*I cannot describe the impression that remained
in my mind after I woke up and found it was
but a dream.*

June 28

*I was somewhat refreshed with sleep
and the fit had passed off. I thought the sick-*

ness might return the next day, so now was the time to get something to support myself in case I should be ill. I filled a square bottle with water, put it within reach of my bed and mixed some rum in it. I made a supper of three turtle eggs, which I roasted in ashes and ate in the shell.

After I had eaten, I tried to walk, but found myself so weak I could hardly carry the gun, and I never went out without that. So I went out only a little way and sat on the ground, looking out on the sea, which was calm and smooth.

After a while I rose, feeling sad, and walked back to my retreat. I had no inclination to sleep, so I sat in my chair and lighted my lamp. I went to find tobacco in one of my chests and took out one of the Bibles, too. I opened the book casually, and the first words that appeared to me were these: "Call on me in the Day of Trouble and I will deliver you and you will glorify me." These words made an impression on me as I read

I HAD NO INCLINATION TO SLEEP,
SO I SAT IN MY CHAIR AND LIGHTED MY LAMP.

them and I often thought about them later.

I am of the opinion that I slept all the next day and night, for otherwise I do not know how I lost a whole day out of my reckoning of the days of the week. When I got up, I was much stronger than the day before, for I was hungry. I had no fit that day and continued much better.

I did not recover my strength for some weeks. The impossibility of being rescued from the island kept me from ever expecting it, but it did occur to me that I had been delivered from sickness. This touched my heart and I knelt down and thanked God for my recovery.

The next morning I began to read the Bible seriously and did so every morning and night. I found my heart was deeply affected by my past wickedness. This was the first time I truly prayed in my life, and I began to have hope that God would hear me. I had a different sense of the captivity I was in. The island was certainly a prison to me, but now I looked back on my past life with such horror that I wished more for deliverance from sin than from suffering.

I had now been on this unhappy island ten months. The possibility of rescue no longer occurred to me and I believed no other human had ever set foot on that place.

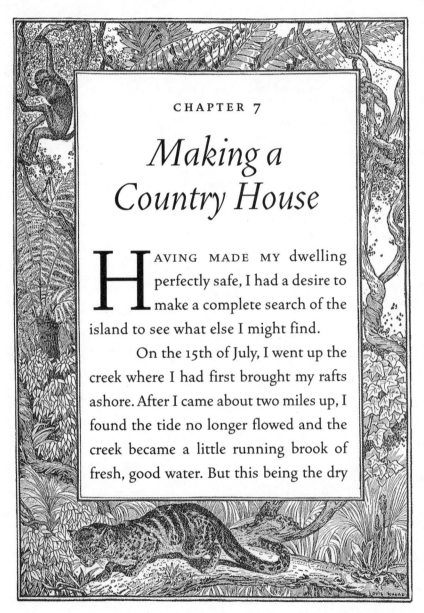

CHAPTER 7

Making a Country House

HAVING MADE MY dwelling perfectly safe, I had a desire to make a complete search of the island to see what else I might find.

On the 15th of July, I went up the creek where I had first brought my rafts ashore. After I came about two miles up, I found the tide no longer flowed and the creek became a little running brook of fresh, good water. But this being the dry season, there was hardly any water in parts of it.

On the bank of the brook I found many pleasant meadows, plain, smooth and covered with grass. On the rising parts of them I found a great deal of tobacco, green and growing to a very great stalk. There were other plants I had no understanding about.

I searched for the cassava root, which the Indians in this climate make their bread out of, but could find none. I saw large plants of aloes but did not then understand them. I saw wild sugar canes.

I came back wondering how I might know the virtues and goodness of the fruits and plants I had found. I had paid so little notice to the plants in the field while I was in Brazil that I did not know how to make them serve me now.

The next day I went the same way, only somewhat farther. The country became more woody. I found melons on the ground and grapes spread over the trees, their clusters very ripe and rich. I was exceedingly glad, but ate sparingly, remembering that eating grapes killed several of our men when they were slaves in Barbary by throwing them into fevers. I found that an excellent use for these grapes was to dry them in the sun as raisins and keep them for when no grapes were to be had.

I spent all that evening there and did not go home, which was the first night I had ever done so. I got up in a tree, where I slept well, and the next morning went on with my discovery, traveling another four miles up the valley. At the end of this march, I came to an opening where the country descended to the west and a spring of fresh water ran the other way to the east. The country appeared so fresh, so green, so flourishing, that it looked like a planted garden.

I went down into this delicious vale, looking on it with a secret kind of pleasure. To think that this was all my own, that I was king of all this country. I saw many cocoa trees, orange, lemon, and lime trees, but few bearing any fruit. The limes I gathered were not only pleasant to eat, but wholesome, and their juice mixed with water was very cool and refreshing.

I now had enough to carry home. I resolved to lay up a store of grapes, limes, and lemons for the wet season, which I knew was near. I gathered a heap of grapes in one place and lemons and limes in another place. Taking a few of each with me, I traveled home. I

I GATHERED A HEAP OF GRAPES IN ONE PLACE
AND LEMONS AND LIMES IN ANOTHER.

intended to come again and bring a sack.

Before I got there, having spent three days on this journey, the grapes spoiled. The ripeness of the fruits made them easily bruised, and they were good for nothing. The next day I went back with two small bags. I was surprised when I came to my heap of grapes to find them all spread about, walked on to pieces and many eaten. I concluded that wild creatures had done this, but I knew not what they were.

Since there was no way to carry the grapes in a sack without them being crushed by their own weight, I hung them in the branches of the trees to dry in the sun. I carried as many lemons and limes back as I could.

When I came home again I thought with pleasure about the fruitfulness of that valley and the safety from storms on that side of the island. I began to consider moving my dwelling.

This thought ran long in my head and I was very fond of it for some time. But when I came to study it closer, I saw that at the seaside something might happen to my advantage. The ill fate that brought me there might bring some other unhappy wretches, too. To enclose myself in the hills and woods of the center of the island made it unlikely that anything might happen for me. Therefore, I decided not to move.

However, I was so fond of the vale that I spent much of my time there, including the whole month of July. I built a bower there, surrounded by a strong fence, like a double hedge filled with brushwood, and stayed two or three nights at a time, always going in it over a ladder. So now I fancied that I had my country house and my seacoast house.

About the beginning of August, I found the grapes I had hung up were indeed dried into excellent raisins. I began to take them down from the trees. I had more than 200 bunches of them, and they were the best part of my winter food. No sooner had I taken them down than it began to rain, which would have spoiled them. It rained more or less every day until the middle of October, sometimes so violently that I could not stir out of my cave for several days.

I had been concerned about the loss of one of my cats, who had run away from me and I thought was dead. To my astonishment, she came home at the end of August with three kittens. This was strange to me because both my cats were females. Later on, I became so pestered with cats that I was forced to kill them and drive them from my house as much as possible.

September 30

I now come to the unhappy anniversary of my landing. I counted up the notches on my post and found I have been here 365 days. I prayed to God to have mercy on me.

A little after this my ink began to fail me, and so I used it only to write down the most remarkable events.

I learned to divide the rainy season and the dry season and prepare for them each. But I paid for my experience before I got it. One of the most discouraging experiments I made was with my few grains of barley and rice. I thought it proper to sow after the rains. Accordingly, I dug up a piece of ground, but as I was sowing, it casually occurred to me not to sow it all at first, so I saved a handful of each.

It was great comfort to me that I did so, for not one grain of what I sowed this time ever came up at all until the wet season came again, and then it grew as if it had just been sown. By this experiment I became the master of my business and knew exactly when the proper time to sow was.

As soon as the rains were over, which was about November, I made a visit up the country to my bower, where I had not been for some months. I found all things as I left them. The hedge I had made was not only firm, but the stakes, which I had cut from trees nearby, were all shot out with long branches. I was surprised and very pleased to see young trees growing. I pruned them and led them to grow as I liked. In three years, they covered a circle 25 yards in diameter in complete shade.

This made me resolve to cut more stakes and make a hedge around the wall of my first dwelling. This I did, placing the stakes about eight yards from my first fence, where they grew and were a fine cover, and later served for a defense also.

After I had learned the ill consequences of being out in the rain, I prepared myself to be indoors as much as possible during the wet months. During this time I had much employment, for I needed a great many things that I could make only by hard labor and constant effort. I tried many ways to make myself a basket, but all the twigs I could get proved too brittle. When I was a boy, I

DURING THE NEXT SEASON I MADE BASKETS.

used to delight in standing by the basket maker in my town and watching the manner in which he worked, sometimes lending a hand. From this, I had full knowledge of the methods of making wicker ware. I wanted nothing but materials. Then it came into my mind that twigs from the tree from which my stakes grew might be as tough as willow.

I went to my country house with a hatchet and cut down plenty of them and set them up to dry. When they were fit, I took them in my cave, and during the next season I made baskets. I did not finish them handsomely, but I made them serve my purpose. Afterwards I took care never to be without them.

Having mastered this difficulty, I stirred myself to see how to supply two things. I had no vessels to hold anything that was liquid, except some glass bottles, but nothing such as a pot to boil things in or make broth. The second thing I wished to have was a tobacco pipe. It was impossible for me to make one, however, at last I found a solution for that, too.

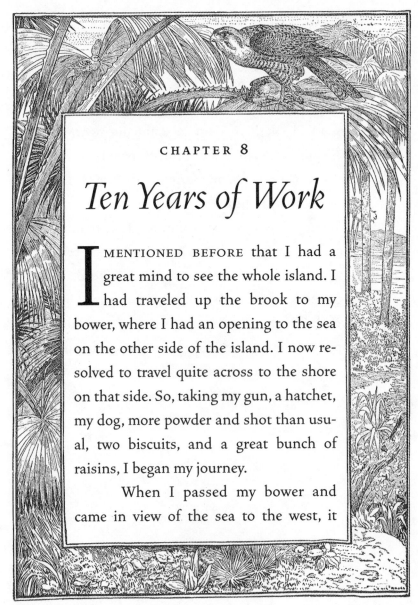

CHAPTER 8

Ten Years of Work

I MENTIONED BEFORE that I had a great mind to see the whole island. I had traveled up the brook to my bower, where I had an opening to the sea on the other side of the island. I now resolved to travel quite across to the shore on that side. So, taking my gun, a hatchet, my dog, more powder and shot than usual, two biscuits, and a great bunch of raisins, I began my journey.

When I passed my bower and came in view of the sea to the west, it being a very clear day, I caught sight of land. I could not tell if it was an island or a continent. But it lay very high and at a great distance. I knew it must be part of America and must be near Spanish lands. Or perhaps it was inhabited by savages.

If this was the Spanish coast, I should certainly, some time or another, see vessels pass. But if not, then it was the savage coast, between Spanish country and Brazil, and the men there were the worst of all savages: cannibals who murder and eat all the humans who fall into their hands.

I found that side of the island was much more pleasant than mine. The open fields were sweet, adorned with flowers, grass, and fine woods. I saw many parrots and I wanted to catch one, keep it to be tame and teach it to speak to me. After some pains, I did knock a young parrot down with a stick, and I brought it home, but it was years before I could make him speak.

Here was also an infinite number of fowl, some of which I had never seen before, and many of them were good meat. I shot as many as I pleased. Though there were more goats here than on my side of the island, it was much more difficult to come near them. Because the country was flat and even, they saw me much sooner.

I traveled along the shore to the east, I suppose about twelve miles, and set up a large pole on the shore for a mark. I decided to go home again and that on the next journey I would come from my dwelling east and so around until I came to my post again.

In this journey, my dog surprised a young kid and seized it. I, running to take hold of it, caught it and saved it alive from the dog. I had a great mind to bring it home if I could, for I had been wondering if it might be possible to raise tame goats to be my food.

I made a collar for this creature and led him along, with some difficulty, until I came to my bower and there I left him. I was impatient to be home, which I had been absent from for a month.

I cannot express how happy I was to come into my old hutch and lie down in my hammock. This wandering journey had been so unsettling, that my own house was a perfect settlement to me. It made everything so comfortable to me that I resolved never to go far from it so long as I had to stay on the island.

I rested myself for a week, during which most of my time was taken up in making a cage for my Poll (as I called my parrot), who began to be tame and well-acquainted with me. Then I thought of the poor kid I had penned in my bower and went to fetch it home. I found it where I left it, but almost starved. I cut branches of such shrubs as I could find and fed it. I tied it to lead it away, but it was so tame with hunger there was no need. It followed me like a dog and, as I continued to feed it, it became so loving, so gentle, and so fond that it would never leave me.

I had been there now two years and had no more prospect of being rescued than the first day I came. But I began to feel how much more happy the life I led now was, even with all its miseries, than that wicked life I led in my past days. My very desires were altered, and my affections changed their directions. Before, as I walked about hunting, the anguish of my situation, how I was a prisoner locked up with the eternal bars of the ocean, would break out on me suddenly. My heart would die within me. I would wring my hands and cry like a child. But now I had new thoughts. Well, then, I said to myself, if God does not forget me, what does it matter that all the world should forget me? I began to think it was possible for me to be more happy alone than I probably would have been in the world. I shocked my mind with that thought. How could I be thankful for a condition that I wished so heartily to be delivered from?

In this frame of mind, I began my third year. I was very seldom idle. Daily tasks, such as going out with my gun, which took three hours every morning, and butchering, preserving and cooking what I killed or caught took up a great part of the day. The heat in the middle of the day was so violent that I could not stir out in it.

To this was added the toil of working without tools, help, or skill, so that everything I did took up time. I spent 42 days to make a long shelf for my cave, which two sawyers could have cut six of from the same tree in half a day. I was three days cutting down the tree and two more cutting off the boughs. With indescribable hacking, I reduced both sides to chips until the log was light enough to move. Then I turned it and made each side smooth until I had a plank about three inches thick. Labor and patience carried me through that and many other things.

I had lost one crop of barley and rice by sowing in the dry season, but my second crop promised very

well. All of a sudden I found I was in danger of losing it
all again. Goats and wild creatures I called hares, tasting
its sweetness, ate the blades so close, as soon as they
came up, that they could get no time to shoot up into
stalks. I saw no remedy but to make a hedge around it.
Since my cropland was small, I got it totally fenced in
three weeks. I shot some of the creatures in daytime and
set my dog to guard at night by tying him to a stake by
the gate, where he barked all night long so that my enemies left the place. In a little time, the grain grew strong
and began to ripen.

But the birds were likely to ruin me now. Going
by my plot to see how it was thriving, I saw my little crop
was surrounded by birds of many sorts, who stood as if
watching for me to leave. I fired among them (for I
always had my gun with me) and there rose up a cloud of
birds I had not seen from among the grain itself. I fore-
saw that in a few days they would devour all my hopes
and that I would be starved.

I went among it to see what damage was done
and found they had spoiled a good deal of it. But it
was yet too green for them. If the remainder could be
saved, it would be a good crop. Coming away, I could

see the thieves sitting in all the trees. I was no sooner out of sight than they dropped down into the grain. I was so provoked that I fired again and killed three of them. I hanged them as we do thieves in England, to scare others. This had such an effect, for the birds would not come at the grain so long as my scarecrows hung there.

I cut my crop as well as I could with a sword I had saved out of the ship, cutting off nothing but the ears of grain and carrying them in one of my baskets. After rubbing the husks off in my hands, I found I had two bushels of rice and two-and-a-half bushels of barley.

Now I was perplexed again, for I knew not how to grind my grain, or make bread of it, or how to bake it. I resolved not to taste this crop but to save it for seed, and in the meantime to study how to accomplish this great work of providing myself with bread. I believe few people have thought of all the many strange little things necessary to making bread.

When it rained and I could not go out, I taught my parrot to speak. He quickly learned his own name and to speak it out pretty loud. "Poll" was the first word

WHEN IT RAINED AND I COULD NOT GO OUT,
I TAUGHT MY PARROT TO SPEAK.

I ever heard on the island by any mouth but my own. Meanwhile my hands were busy. I had long studied how to make myself some pottery. If I could find some clay, I might **botch up** some pot that, dried in the sun, would be hard enough to hold things that were dry, such as flour.

BOTCH UP
Make clumsily.

The reader would laugh at the odd, ugly things I made and how many of them fell in. Many were cracked by the heat of the sun or fell to pieces when I picked them up. In two months of labor, I could make but two ugly earthen things. I cannot call them jars. However, these two I set inside wicker baskets, which I made on purpose to protect the pots.

I made smaller pots with better success, but none of these would answer my aim, which was to have an earthen pot that would hold liquid and bear the fire. It happened once that, after making a big fire to cook my meat, I found in the embers a broken piece of one of my pots, burnt as hard as stone. This set me to studying how to burn my pots. I placed three large pots in a pile and placed firewood all around it. I fed the fire with fuel until I saw the pots inside glow red-hot and then clear red through. I let them stand in that heat for six hours, until

I FOUND CLAY AND LEARNED TO MAKE POTS THAT I COULD
USE TO HOLD LIQUID AND BEAR THE FIRE.

one began to melt, and then I slackened the fire off. I watched them all night, so that the fire did not die too fast, and in the morning had three very good, though not handsome, pots. No joy was ever equal to mine when I found my earthen pot would bear the fire. Now I could boil meat and make broth.

All the while I was doing these things, I thought many times of the distant land I had seen from the other side of the island. I had secret wishes to be on that shore. I fancied that from there I might find some way or other to get farther and perhaps at last escape.

I gave no thought to the danger in going there, or how I might fall into the hands of Caribbean savages, who I had heard were cannibals. Even if they were not man-eaters, they might still kill me, as had happened to many Europeans. All these fears came to me later, but not at first.

I wished I had Xury and the long boat we sailed for a thousand miles along the coast of Africa. Then I thought of our ship's boat, which was blown up on the shore with its bottom side up. She would have done well enough, but I could not turn her over any better than I could move the island. However, I tried with levers and digging away sand

and spared no pains in this fruitless effort. After four weeks I was forced to give up on the boat.

Next, I began to wonder if I could make a canoe such as the natives make, by hollowing out the trunk of a tree. I thought it would be easy. But I did not consider the difficulty, once it was made, of moving it to the water. I went to work on the boat the most like a fool of any man who ever had his senses awake. I was very pleased with my plan, even though I did not know if I could accomplish it. I said to myself, make it and then find some way to get it along.

I eagerly went to work and felled a cedar tree. It was five feet, ten inches in diameter at the stump and four feet, eleven inches in diameter at the end of 22 feet, where the trunk parted in branches. I spent twenty days hacking at the bottom and fourteen more days getting off the limbs. It cost me a month to shape the outside to something like a boat, so that it would float upright. It cost me three months more to clear out the inside. I did this without fire, just a mallet and chisel and hard labor. In the end, I had a very handsome canoe that would have carried 26 men, big enough for me and all my cargo. It had cost many a weary stroke.

There remained nothing but to get it in the water. It lay about 100 yards from the creek, with a hill in the way. I dug away the surface, but could no more stir the canoe than I could the other boat. Then I resolved to cut a canal to bring the water to the canoe. Well, I began this work and when I understood how deep and how broad it would need to be, I found it would take ten or twelve years to do. Now I saw the folly of beginning the work before we count the cost and judge rightly our own strength to go through with it.

In the middle of this work, I finished my fourth year in this place. I had gained a different knowledge than I had before. I now looked upon the world as something remote, which I had nothing to do with. I was removed from the wickedness of the world here. I had neither lust nor pride. There was nothing to covet. I was king over the whole country and had no rivals.

My experience showed me that all the things of this world are only good so far as we can use them and, however many things we may heap up, we enjoy just as much as we can use, and no more. I had no benefit from the parcel of money I had; it grew moldy in the damp of the cave. I would have given it all for a dozen tobacco pipes or a handmill to grind grain, or a handful of beans and peas, or a bottle of ink. And if I had a drawer full of diamonds, it would have been the same; they had no value to me because they had no use.

My state of life now was much easier to my mind. I learned to look more on the bright side of my condition and consider what I had, rather than what I wanted. All our discontent about what we want springs from our ingratitude for what we have.

I had been on the island so long that many things I had brought ashore were gone or almost worn out. My ink had been gone for some time. My clothes began to decay, too. The weather was so violently hot that there was no need of clothes, yet I could not go naked. I could not even stand to think of it, though I was all alone. The reason was I could not bear the heat of the sun, which blistered my skin and gave me headaches. If I went out in a shirt and wearing a hat I was twice as cool as without them.

I saved the skins of the four-footed creatures I killed and stretched them out in the sun. Some were so dry and hard they were fit for little, but others were useful. The first thing I made was a cap for my head, with

AFTER THIS I SPENT A GREAT DEAL OF TIME
AND PAINS TO MAKE AN UMBRELLA.

the fur on the outside to shed rain. After this I made a suit of clothes, a loose coat and britches that came to the knee, both also with the fur on the outside. They were wretchedly made, for I was an even worse tailor than I was a carpenter. However, if it happened to rain, they kept me very dry.

After this I spent a great deal of time and pains to make an umbrella. I had a great want of one and had seen them made in Brazil, where they are useful against the heat. I took a world of trouble with it and spoiled two or three before I made one to my mind. The main difficulty I had was to make it let down. But at last, I had one to work and covered it with skins.

Thus I lived comfortably, my mind at ease by resigning to the will of God.

For five years after this, nothing extraordinary happened. Besides my plantings, I had one labor, digging the canal, six feet wide and four feet deep, to bring my canoe to the creek, almost a half a mile away. I never grudged the labor because of the hope it gave me of going off to sea at last.

However, once it was finished, the smallness of my canoe put an end to my design of venturing to the land I had seen 40 miles away. I thought no more of it. My next plan was to make a tour around the island.

I fitted a mast and sail to my boat and found she sailed very well. I made lockers at either end to hold provisions dry from the spray of the sea and cut a hollow place along the inside where I could lay my gun, hanging a flap over it to keep it dry. I fixed my umbrella at the stern, like an awning, to keep the sun off me.

Every now and then I took a little voyage, but never far out or far from my little creek. At last, being eager to tour my kingdom, I supplied my ship with food for the voyage, putting in two dozen loaves of barley bread, a pot of toasted rice, a little rum, half a goat, powder, shot, and two coats to cover me in the night.

I found this voyage much longer than expected. Though the island was not large, when I came to the east side of it, I found a great ledge of rocks that stretched two leagues out to sea, some above water, some under it. Beyond that was a shoal of sand lying dry for half a league more, so that I was forced to go a great way out to sea to get around the point.

I thought of giving up my enterprise, not knowing how far it might take me out to sea and doubting that

I should ever get back again. So I came to an anchor, took my gun, and went on shore, climbing up a hill that overlooked the point. When I saw the full extent of it, I decided to venture on.

I waited there two days for the wind to calm and then set out. But no sooner did I reach the point, not even my boat's length from it, than I found myself in a great depth of water and in a current like a **millrace**. It carried my boat along with such violence that I found myself hurried farther and farther out to sea. There was no wind to help me, and all I could do with my paddles achieved nothing. I began to give myself up as lost. I knew soon the current would carry me leagues distant into the vast ocean and I had no possibility of avoiding it. I would perish by the sea or from starving.

MILLRACE
The fast-moving stream of water that turns a mill wheel.

Now I saw how easy it is that the most miserable things can become worse. I looked back at my desolate, solitary island as the most pleasant place in the world, and all my heart wished for was just to be there again. I scolded myself for my unthankful temper. We never know how to value what we enjoy, except by the lack of it.

However, I worked hard, with all my strength, to keep my boat toward the side of the current and about noon I felt a little breeze in my face. This cheered me a little. By this time I was a frightful distance from the island and should never have known which way to steer if I lost sight of it. I set up my mast and spread my sail to the breeze.

As my boat began to stretch away, the current weakened, and as I steered to the east I found another current. I turned my sail to it and ran cheerfully before the wind, with a strong tide underneath, directly toward the island. I found myself open to the northern shore, opposite to the part of the island I had set out from. About four o'clock in the evening, I got to land.

When I was on shore, I fell on my knees and thanked God for delivering me. I laid aside all thoughts of escaping the island by my boat. I brought my boat close by in a little cove, under some trees, and laid down to sleep, quite spent with labor and fatigue.

I was at a loss over which way to get home with my boat. I knew the hazard of attempting it by the way I first went out. I had not the mind to make any more adventures, and in the morning I resolved to make my

way westward. After about three miles coasting along
the shore, I came to a good inlet and found a conve-
nient harbor for my boat, where she lay as if in a dock
made on purpose for her. I stowed her very safe and
went on shore to see where I was.

I found I was but a little way from the place
where I had traveled on foot before. So, taking nothing out of my boat but my gun and umbrella, I began
my march. I reached my old bower in the evening and
found everything in good order as I had left it.

I got over the fence, laid myself down in the
shade to rest and fell asleep. What a surprise I was in
when I was awakened by a voice calling me by my name
several times: Robin, Robin, Robin, Robinson Crusoe.
Poor Robin Crusoe. Where are you, Robin Crusoe?

I was so dead asleep, so tired from rowing and
walking, that I did not wake thoroughly. I thought I
dreamed that somebody spoke to me. But as the voice
repeated Robin Crusoe, Robin Crusoe, at last I sat up
in confusion. I saw my Poll sitting on top of the hedge
and immediately knew it was he that spoke to me. It
was in such bemoaning language that I used to talk to
him, and he had learned it perfectly.

I held out my hand and called him by his name. The friendly creature came to me and sat upon my thumb, as he used to do, and continued talking to me, saying, "Poor Robin Crusoe," and "How did I come here?" and "Where have I been?" It was as if he were overjoyed to see me again, and so I carried him home with me.

I had now had enough of rambling to sea. I would have been very glad to have my boat on my side of the island, but I knew not how to get it there. I supposed the current ran with the same force along the west shore as it did on the east, and I might run the same risk of being carried away from the island by venturing that way. With these thoughts, I contented myself to be without my boat, even though it had taken so many months to make it, and so many more to get it into the sea.

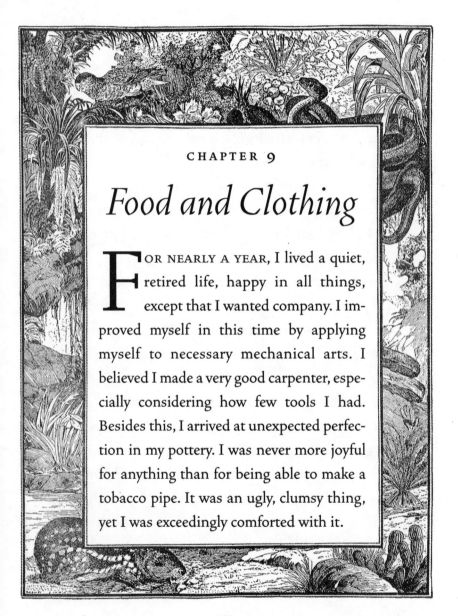

CHAPTER 9

Food and Clothing

FOR NEARLY A YEAR, I lived a quiet, retired life, happy in all things, except that I wanted company. I improved myself in this time by applying myself to necessary mechanical arts. I believed I made a very good carpenter, especially considering how few tools I had. Besides this, I arrived at unexpected perfection in my pottery. I was never more joyful for anything than for being able to make a tobacco pipe. It was an ugly, clumsy thing, yet I was exceedingly comforted with it.

My supply of powder had been considerably reduced. I began to think seriously of what I would do when I ran out. How would I kill a goat? Since my third year here, I had kept a kid and made her tame, but could not get a he-goat. I could never find it in my heart to kill her and at last she died of old age.

I set myself to study the art of trapping goats, particularly a she-goat great with young. I made snares, but I always found them broken and my bait eaten. I decided to try a pitfall and so dug several large pits where I saw the goats feed and covered them with twigs. Many times I found my traps still standing, yet the bait was eaten. This was very discouraging. However, one morning I found in one of them a large old he-goat and three kids, two females and one male.

I knew not what to do with the old one, so I let him out and he ran away as if frightened out of his wits. I forgot that hunger will tame a lion. If I had let him stay there four days without food and then carried him water to drink, he would have been as tame as one of the kids, for they are wise creatures when they are well-treated. I tied the kids together with strings and with some difficulty got them all home.

NOW I HAD NOT ONLY MEAT, BUT MILK TOO,
WHICH IN THE BEGINNING I DID NOT THINK OF.

Then it occurred to me that to keep them from running wild when they grew up, I must enclose some piece of ground. This was a great undertaking for one pair of hands, yet I saw it was necessary. For the beginning, I decided to enclose a piece about 150 yards long and 100 yards wide. As my flock increased I would add more ground. I was about three months hedging the first piece, and until I had it done I tethered the three kids. I fed them rice and barley out of my hands, so that after they were loose they would follow me bleating for a handful of grain.

In about a year-and-a-half, I had a flock of twelve goats, and in two years I had 43, besides several I killed for food. I enclosed five pieces of ground for them, with little pens and gates out of one to another. Now I had not only meat, but milk too, which in the beginning I did not think of. I set up a dairy and sometimes had a gallon or two of milk in a day. After many attempts, at last I made butter and cheese and never lacked for them again.

It would make a **stoic** smile to see me and my little family

STOIC
Someone who does not show passion and tries to appear untouched by pleasure or pain is a stoic. The term comes from a philosophy about virtue and wisdom begun by Zeno, a Greek, that later became popular with the Romans.

sit down to dinner. I was the prince and lord of the whole island. I had the lives of all my subjects at my command. I could give liberty or take it away, and I had no rebels among my subjects.

Like a king, I too dined all alone. Poll was the only one permitted to talk to me. My dog, now grown old and crazy, sat always at my right hand, and two cats sat one on each side of the table, expecting tidbits from my hand.

I was impatient to have my boat, but afraid to run any more risks. Sometimes I tried to think of ways to get her, and other times I was content to be without her. I had a strange uneasiness in my mind about the point of the island that I once went up the hill to see. This feeling increased every day until finally I decided to travel there by following the shore.

For five or six days I traveled along the sea to the place where I first brought out my boat. From there I went over land a shorter way to the height I had climbed before and looked out to the point of rocks. I was surprised to see the sea smooth, no rippling, no currents. I was at a loss to understand this and decided to spend time watching it to see if the changing of the tide was the cause. By evening I was convinced it was. By studying the tide I could easily bring my boat around the island again. But when I thought about actually doing it, I had such a terror at remembering the danger I had been in that I decided instead to make another canoe. So I would have one for one side of the island and one for the other.

You must understand I now had two plantations, as I called them, on my island. One was my little fort with the cave behind it, which I had enlarged to several rooms. My wall had grown into trees spread so big that no one could have seen my home behind them. Near this dwelling lay my two pieces of cropland.

Besides this I had my country home, my bower, as I called it. I kept the trees cut to grow thick and wild, to make more shade. Inside their hedge, which now formed a strong wall, I had my tent made from a sail. Nearby I had my pastures for my goats. This shows I was not idle.

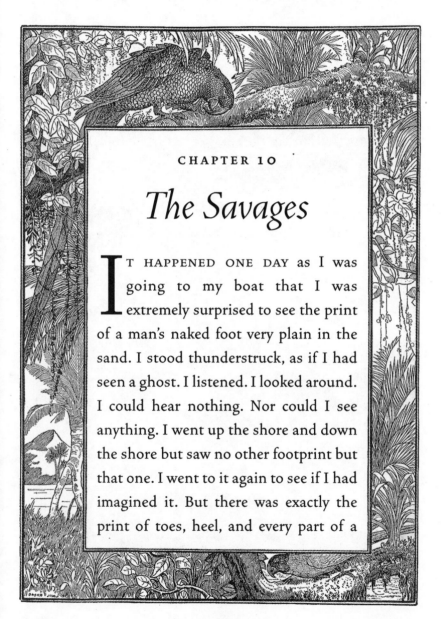

CHAPTER 10

The Savages

I T HAPPENED ONE DAY as I was going to my boat that I was extremely surprised to see the print of a man's naked foot very plain in the sand. I stood thunderstruck, as if I had seen a ghost. I listened. I looked around. I could hear nothing. Nor could I see anything. I went up the shore and down the shore but saw no other footprint but that one. I went to it again to see if I had imagined it. But there was exactly the print of toes, heel, and every part of a

I WAS EXTREMELY SURPRISED TO SEE THE PRINT
OF A MAN'S NAKED FOOT VERY PLAIN IN THE SAND.

foot. I knew not how it came to be there.

With many confused thoughts I came home to my fort, not feeling the ground I was walking on, looking behind me every two or three steps, and imagining every bush and tree in the distance to be a man.

When I came to my castle, for that is what I called it from then on, I fled into it like a rabbit runs for cover. I did not sleep that night. How was it possible that a man came there? It must be some savages from the mainland who wandered over the sea in their canoes had been on shore and gone to sea again.

Terrible thoughts racked my mind over whether they found my boat and knew people were here. If so, they would certainly come again in greater numbers and eat me. And if they could not find me, they would find my home and take my grain and carry away my goats, and I would starve. My fear banished all my hope.

How strange is the life of man! Today we love what tomorrow we hate. Today we seek what tomorrow we shun. Today we want what tomorrow we fear. While I was alone, cut off from mankind, I would have thought I was raised from death to life to see another man. But now I trembled with fear at the silent shadow of a man putting his foot on the island. Fears took up my thoughts and I prayed to God to deliver me.

One day it came to me that perhaps all this was a delusion. The footprint might have come from my own foot once when I came on shore from my boat. This cheered me up a little. Now I began to take courage and peep out again. I had not left my castle for three days. I had no more food indoors, only water, and I knew my goats wanted to be milked.

So I went out for two or three days to my country bower and, having seen nothing, I became bolder. Yet, I could not persuade myself I was deluded until I went to the shore and measured the print against my own foot. When I came to the place, I saw I could not possibly have come on shore anywhere near there and that my foot was a great deal smaller than the print. I shook again with cold and went home, filled with the belief that some man or men had been on shore. I knew not what to do to be safe.

I considered it most likely that the landing was accidental. Straggling people from the mainland were probably driven to the island against their will and they

I MADE AN OUTER WALL AROUND MY DWELLNG, THICKENED
WITH PIECES OF TIMBER. I PUT SEVEN HOLES IN IT
AND FITTED MUSKETS AT THE HOLES.

went off again with all possible speed, not staying the night. Therefore I need only have a safe retreat in case I should see any savages land.

So now I made an outer wall around my dwelling, thickened with pieces of timber. I put seven holes in it, about big enough to stick my arm through. I fitted muskets at the holes, like a cannon, so that I could fire all seven guns in two minutes. Outside the wall I stuck sticks that would take root. So in five years' time I had woods in front of my home so thick and strong that it was impassable. No man could have imagined anything was behind it. I left no way in or out except for my ladder, which if I took down, no man could reach me.

While I was doing this, I had a concern for my goats. I did not want to lose them. I could think of two ways to save them. One was to find a cave and drive them in it every night. The other was to enclose two or three bits of land, far from each other and hidden as much as possible, and put a dozen goats in each. This second plan I thought was the best.

I spent some time to find the most remote part of the island. In thick woods where I had almost lost myself once before, I found a clear piece of land, nearly three acres large. I immediately went to work on it and in less than a month had it fenced around. Without delay, I put twelve young goats in it.

All this labor was on account of one man's footprint, for I had never seen any human come near the island. I had lived two years under this uneasiness, which made my life uncomfortable. Every night I expected to be murdered and eaten before morning.

After I had made one part of my goats safe, I went about the island looking for another private place to make another such enclosure. Wandering to the western point of the island, where I had never been before, and looking out to sea, I thought I saw a boat in the distance. I did not have my spyglass with me. I could not tell whether it was a boat or not, but I descended the hill and could not see it any longer. I decided not to go out again without my spyglass.

When I came down the hill to the shore, I was amazed and horrified to see the shore spread with skulls, hands, feet, and other bones. I observed a place where a fire had been made and a circle dug out of the earth where savages had sat down to feast on the bodies of their fellow creatures.

I WAS AMAZED AND HORRIFIED TO SEE THE SHORE SPREAD
WITH SKULLS, HANDS, FEET AND OTHER BONES.

I was so astonished at this sight I did not think of danger to myself. My fears were buried by thoughts of inhuman brutality, which I had never had so near a view of before. I turned my face from the spectacle and my stomach grew sick. I vomited with uncommon violence and felt a little better, but could not bear to stay in that place another moment. So I climbed up the hill with all the speed I could and walked on home. With a flood of tears in my eyes, I thanked God that I had been born in a part of the world where I was different from such dreadful creatures.

In this mood of thankfulness I went to my castle. I began to feel much easier now about my safety, for I saw that the savages never came to the island in search of anything. I had been here eighteen years and never saw a footstep and might stay another eighteen, hidden as I was now, if I did not reveal myself to them.

Yet I felt such horror at the savages and their custom of eating their own, that I kept to myself for two years. I was as fearful of seeing these hellish wretches as of seeing the devil himself. I did not go look at my boat in all this time. Nor could I think of bringing it around the island for fear of meeting these creatures at sea. If ever I happened to fall into their hands, I knew what my fate would be.

Time, however, began to wear off my uneasiness about these people. I began to live in the same calm manner as before, only I kept my eyes more about me and I was more cautious about firing my gun in case any of them were on the island and might happen to hear it. I did not fire it for two years, though I never went out without it. I always carried three pistols in my belt and a broad cutlass hanging at my side.

Night and day, I could think of nothing else but how I might destroy some of these monsters at their bloody entertainment and, if possible, save their victim. But what could one man do when there might be 20 or 30 of them with their bows and arrows? I thought of waiting in ambush for them, with my guns double-loaded, and shooting them in the middle of their ceremony. Then I would fall on them with my sword and kill them all. I was so full of this idea that I often dreamed it.

I found a place on the side of a hill where I felt I could safely wait until I saw their boats coming. Then, before they got to shore, I could move unseen to a thicket of trees, one of which was hollow and large enough to conceal me entirely. There I could sit and aim at their heads and not fail to wound three or four of them with the first shot. I prepared two muskets and a fowling piece with handfuls of shot. I also loaded my pistols with four bullets each.

Every morning I made a tour to the top of the hill, which was about three miles from my castle, to look for ships on the sea. But I began to tire of this duty after two or three months. I never made any discovery on the whole ocean as far as my spyglass could reach. I began to be weary of the trip and my opinion of my plan began to change. What right had I to be the judge and executioner of these men?

Next it occurred to me that the brutal way they treated each other was really nothing to me. These people had done me no harm. They had no knowledge of me, therefore it would be unjust for me to attack them. I concluded that my business was to conceal myself from them, and that I was wrong to lay schemes for their destruction. For a year after this, I never once went up the hill to see if any of them were in sight or had been there. All I did was move my boat down to the east where I knew they would never come because of the currents.

I was uneasy about making fires. The smoke, which could be seen at a great distance, might betray me. So I began to make charcoal to burn because it had no danger from smoke. One day while I was cutting thick branches to make charcoal, by sheer accident I found a natural cave where no man, no savage would go in, unless he needed a safe hiding place.

I was curious to look and got in with difficulty. It was pretty large, open enough for me to stand up in. But I made haste to get out because when I looked farther into the place, I saw two shining eyes of some creature, twinkling like two stars in the dim light.

Plucking up my courage, I took up a flaming stick from the fire and went in again. I had not gone three steps when I heard a loud sigh, like a man in pain. Then came a noise that sounded like words half-spoken. I stepped back and began to sweat. It seemed as if my hair was lifting the hat off my head. But, plucking up my courage again, I stepped forward and by the light of the firebrand I saw on the ground a frightful old he-goat gasping and dying of old age.

I stirred him to see if I could get him out, and he tried to get up, but he could not raise himself. He died the next day, and I buried him in the cave. I decided to store some of my guns and gunpowder there as my place of last retreat. Five hundred savages could never find me there.

I was now in my twenty-third year of living on the island. It was the time of my harvest, and I was often out in my fields. Going out pretty early one morning, before daylight, I was surprised to see the light of a fire on the shore.

I feared that if the savages rambled over the island and found my grain fields or my other improvements, they would never give up looking for me until they found me. In this state of worry I went back to my castle and pulled in the ladder. I prepared to defend myself to my last gasp. I loaded all the muskets on my fort and my pistols. I sat in readiness for two hours, impatient to know what was happening on the shore.

When I could bear my ignorance no longer, I climbed to the top of the hill above my castle. I laid down flat on the ground and took out my spyglass. I saw nine naked savages sitting around a fire, which I supposed they made, not to stay warm, because the weather was hot, but to cook human flesh. Whether their meal was alive or dead I did not know. They had

I LAID DOWN FLAT ON THE GROUND AND TOOK OUT MY SPYGLASS.
I SAW NINE NAKED SAVAGES SITTING AROUND A FIRE.

two canoes with them, which they had hauled on shore. They seemed to be waiting for the high tide in order to leave.

As I expected, so it happened. As soon as the tide came from the west, they all took to their boats and paddled away. For the hour or so before they went off, they had been dancing. I could see that they were naked, but I could not tell if they were men or women.

As soon as they were gone I took two guns on my

shoulders, two pistols in my belt, and my sword and went to the hill where I had first discovered them. I was so loaded down it took me two hours to get there. Looking out from there, I found three more canoes of savages taking to sea together.

This was a dreadful sight to me. Going down to the shore, I saw marks of horror. Their work left blood, bones, and parts of human flesh where they had eaten with merriment. I was filled with disgust and began to plan again the destruction of whomever I might find there.

It seemed clear to me that these visits were not very frequent. It was fifteen months before I saw any sign of the savages again. All this time I was in a killing mood and took up time, which should have been better spent, trying to think of how to murder them.

In the middle of May of that year, according to my wooden calendar, there was a great storm with lightning, thunder, and a very foul night. As I sat thinking of my troubles, I was surprised to hear the noise of a gun fired at sea. I climbed immediately to the top of my hill. As I got there, I saw a flash of fire and in a moment heard the sound of a second gun. I knew this was the signal of a ship in distress. I brought together all the dry wood I could find and set it on fire on the top of the hill. The wood blazed freely and I have no doubt the ship saw it, for as soon as my fire blazed up I heard several more guns from the same direction. I kept the fire burning all night long, and when day broke I could see something at a great distance on the sea, a hull or a sail, I could not tell which.

I ran to the south side of the island, toward the rocks the current had carried me away to. Getting there, I could plainly see, to my great sorrow, the wreck of a ship on those rocks. I cannot explain by words the longing of my soul that one or two souls out of that ship might be saved to become a companion to me. "O, had there been but one," I repeated to myself a thousand times, with my fingers pressing into the palms of my hands and my teeth set strong against each other.

But it was not to be. Some days later the body of a drowned boy washed ashore. He had no clothes on but a seaman's blue shirt and pants. He had nothing in his pocket but two gold coins and a tobacco pipe.

Meanwhile, the weather was calm and I had a mind to venture out to the wreck in my boat. I had no doubt I would find something that might be useful to me. More important, there might yet be a living creature on board whose life I could save and thus bring comfort to myself. This thought was so strong on my mind that I believed I should be wrong if I did not go.

I loaded my boat with fresh water, bread, a compass, rum, raisins, goat's milk and cheese, and my umbrella and launched into the ocean. I felt the benefit of the current, which carried me directly to the wreck in less than two hours.

It was a dismal sight. The ship, which looked Spanish, was stuck between two rocks, all beaten to pieces. As I came close a dog appeared, crying and yelping, and jumped into the sea. I took him in my boat and gave him water and a cake of bread, which he ate like a wolf that had been starving in the snow.

After this I went on board. The first sight I had was of two drowned men, their arms tight around each other. Besides the dog, there was nothing left alive. Nor were there any goods not spoiled by water. I saw several chests belonging to seamen and I got two of them in my boat. From what I found in these chests, I supposed the ship had a good deal of wealth on board and that she may have been bound for Buenos Aires or Havana or perhaps Spain. But her treasure was of no use to anybody. For now, I knew not what became of the rest of her people.

Besides the chests, I found twenty gallons of liquor, four pounds of gunpowder, fire tongs and a grate, and brass and copper kettles, all of which I loaded in my boat. The tide now running toward home, I left the wreck and reached the island at dusk, very weary.

I slept that night in the boat and in the morning carried my cargo to my cave, not to my castle. In the chests I found some very good shirts, a case of bottles filled with fine liqueurs, handkerchiefs, and eleven-hundred **pieces of eight** as well as six gold bars. On the whole, I got little from my voyage. The money meant as much to me as the dirt under my feet. I would have given it all for a pair of shoes and some stockings. However, I did lug it all to my cave.

PIECES OF EIGHT
Spanish gold coins.

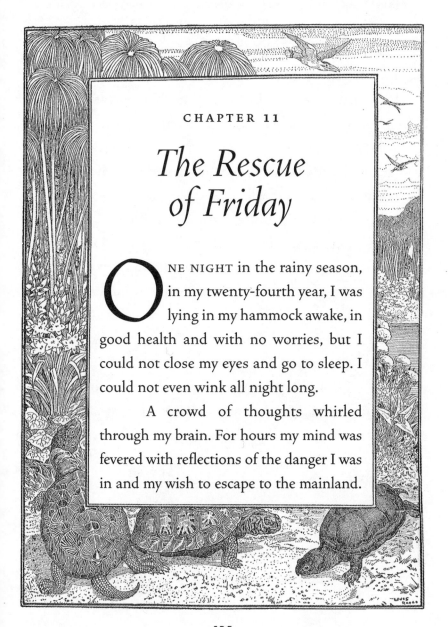

CHAPTER 11

The Rescue of Friday

ONE NIGHT in the rainy season, in my twenty-fourth year, I was lying in my hammock awake, in good health and with no worries, but I could not close my eyes and go to sleep. I could not even wink all night long.

A crowd of thoughts whirled through my brain. For hours my mind was fevered with reflections of the danger I was in and my wish to escape to the mainland.

The worst that could happen in the attempt would be that I would die, but that would only end my misery. Exhausted by being upset, at last I fell asleep and had a dream.

I dreamed that as I was going out in the morning, as usual, I saw on the shore two canoes. Eleven savages had landed and brought another savage whom they meant to kill and eat. All of a sudden, that savage jumped and ran for his life into my thick little grove. I showed myself to him and smiled to him. He kneeled down and seemed to pray to me to help him. I showed him the ladder into my castle and made him go in. He became my servant, and I said to myself that now I will certainly reach the mainland because this fellow will know how to take me there.

I woke from this dream with a feeling of joy at the prospect of escape, but finding that it was only a dream, I became very dejected. However, from this I concluded that I must try to get a savage in my possession. If possible, it should be one of their prisoners. I trembled at the difficulty of attacking them all and shedding so much blood. This was desperate and might go wrong. I had many disputes with myself over it, but at last I resolved to try to do it, whatever it cost.

With this resolution I set myself to scout as often as possible. For a year-and-a-half I waited, looking almost every day for canoes. But none appeared.

Then early one morning I was surprised to see five canoes, all on shore on my side of the island. The people had all landed and gone out of sight. I could not think of how to attack 20 or 30 men singlehandedly, so I stayed still in my castle, confused and upset. I prepared my castle for defense and waited a good while. Then, being impatient, I climbed up on my hill. With my spyglass I could see 30 savages, dancing around a fire.

While I watched, two miserable souls were dragged from the boats and brought out for slaughter. One was knocked down immediately with a wooden club, and three savages went to work cutting him open. The other was left standing by until they were ready for him. At this moment, that poor wretch, seeing himself left alone, and with the hope of life, bolted from them and ran with incredible swiftness along the sand in the direction of my home.

I was very frightened to see him run my way. But only three men followed him, and he ran so fast I could see that, if he could keep it up, he would get away from them all. My dream was coming to pass. Between them and my castle was the creek where I landed my cargos. The wretch must swim there or be taken again. When he came to it, he plunged in and swam. Reaching the other side, he ran on with strength and speed. Two of those chasing could swim, but they took twice as long to get over the creek. The third turned and went back.

It came to me plainly that I was called by Providence to save this poor creature's life. I ran down and fetched my two guns and made haste, by a short cut, all the way down the hill. I came out between the escaping savage and his pursuers. I called to the man fleeing to come to me, but he looked at me with as much fright as he had of those chasing him. But again I waved to him with my hand to come back. I turned on the two that followed and charged and struck the first with the **stock** of my gun. I did not want to fire it for fear the other savages could hear.

STOCK
The part of a gun to which the barrel is attached.

When I knocked the one fellow down, the other stopped, as if he was scared. I went towards him and, as I came near, I saw he had a bow and arrow and was preparing to shoot at me. This forced me to shoot at him first, which I did, and I killed him on the first shot. The poor savage stopped fleeing when he saw his enemies dead. He was so afraid of the fire and noise of my gun he stood still, though he seemed to want to continue running. He feared I meant to kill him as I had the others.

I hollered to him to come on and made signs that he understood. He came a little way and stopped. Then he came a little further and stopped. He knelt down every ten or twelve steps to acknowledge me for saving his life. I smiled at him pleasantly to encourage him. Finally he came close to me and knelt down again, kissed the ground, and laid his head on it. Then he took my foot and set it on his head. This was his way of swearing to be my slave. I raised him up and made much over him.

Now I saw that the one I had knocked down was not dead, but only stunned. So I pointed to him and the savage said some words to me. Though I did not understand them, they were pleasant to hear, for they were the first human sounds I had heard, except for my own, in 25 years. Now the fellow sat up and my savage, as I called him, became afraid. I pointed my gun at the man. Now my savage pointed at my sword. So I lent it to him. He no sooner had it than he ran to his enemy and in one blow

FINALLY HE CAME CLOSE TO ME, KNELT DOWN, AND KISSED THE
GROUND. THEN HE TOOK MY FOOT AND SET IT ON HIS HEAD.

neatly cut off his head. He came back to me laughing, making signs of triumph and many other gestures. He brought the head of the man he killed to me and put it and the sword down in front of me.

He seemed astonished that I had killed the other Indian so far off. So I made signs to him to go look. He stood over the man amazed, turning the body from one side to the other, looking at the wound the bullet made and the great amount of blood. I made signs for him to follow me, fearing others might come. But he made signs back that we should bury them, so the others would not find them. I made a sign to him to do so. He fell to it and in an instant scraped a hole in the sand, dragged a man in and covered him. Then he did the same to the second. He buried them both in a quarter of an hour. Then I took him to my secret cave.

Here I gave him bread and raisins to eat, and water, which he wanted greatly because of his running. He lay down on a pile of rice straw and went to sleep. He was a handsome fellow, not too large, tall and well-built, and I estimated about 26 years old. His face was not fierce or mean, but manly, with a sweet and soft expression when he smiled. His hair was long and black and not curly. His eyes had a sparkling sharpness. His skin was tawny. His head was round, his nose small, and he had fine white teeth.

After a half-hour slumber, he awoke and came out of the cave to where I was milking my goats. He lay down beside me and made all possible signs of humble thanks. Then he put his head on the ground and, as he had done before, put my foot on his head to show his submission to me. I understood many of his gestures and let him know I was pleased with him.

I began to speak to him and to teach him how to speak to me. First I made him know his name would be Friday, which was the day I saved his life. I likewise taught him to say master and that that was my name. I taught him the meaning of yes and no. And I showed him how to eat a cake of bread sopped in goat's milk.

The next day as we went by the place where he had buried the two men, Friday pointed to the graves and made signs that we should dig them up and eat them. I was very angry and expressed my disgust at it. I acted as if I would vomit and beckoned to him to come away, which he did meekly. We went to the top of the hill where, with my spyglass, I saw that the savages had left without making any search for their two comrades.

Now with more courage and curiosity, we marched to where the savages had been. My blood ran chill in my veins. My heart sank at the horror of the spectacle. It was dreadful to me, though Friday thought nothing of it. The place was covered with bones and the ground was dyed with blood. Great pieces of flesh, scorched and mangled, were left here and there, the signs of a feast of victory over their enemies. I counted three skulls, five hands, and the bones of four legs and feet and many other parts. Friday, by signs, made me understand that there had been four prisoners here from a battle between his king and a neighboring king. Many prisoners, of which he was one, had been taken to many places in order to feast on them.

I made Friday gather all the bones and flesh in a heap, make a fire and burn everything to ashes. I saw he hankered to eat some of the flesh and was still a cannibal in his nature. But I made plain my hatred of it and let him know I would kill him if he showed signs of it.

When we had done this we went back to the castle to find Friday clothes, for he was stark naked. I gave him a pair of pants from a seaman's chest and made him

I GAVE HIM A PAIR OF PANTS FROM A SEAMAN'S CHEST
AND MADE HIM A GOATSKIN VEST.

a goatskin vest. I also gave him a cap made of rabbit skin.
He was mighty pleased to see himself almost as well-
clothed as his master. He was awkward in his things at
first, and he complained that they hurt him. But after he
wore them for a while, he took to them very well.

I began to consider where he would lodge. I made
a little tent for him between the inner and outer walls of
my fort. I made a formal door that I could bar at night for
the passage to my cave. When I took in my ladders too,

Friday could not come at me inside my dwelling without making so much noise that I would be awakened. I put all my weapons by my side at night.

I needed none of these precautions, however. No man ever had a more faithful and loving servant than Friday was to me. He was without moods or schemes and was as affectionate to me as a child is to his father. He would have sacrificed his life to save mine at any time. I was soon convinced I did not need to fear for my safety from him.

In fact, I was very delighted with my new companion and worked to teach him everything useful, especially to speak to me. He was an able student, merry and hard working, and so pleased when we could understand each other. My life became so easy that I said to myself I no longer cared if I left the island.

To end Friday's cannibal ways, I thought I ought to let him taste other meat. So I took him out one morning to kill a kid from my flock. I saw a goat with two kids beside her lying in the shade and, motioning to Friday to stand still, I shot and killed one of the kids. Poor Friday did not understand how it was done and was shaking and amazed. He had not seen the kid I shot at and so tore off his shirt to see if he was wounded. He thought that I meant to kill him. He kneeled down and hugged my knees, saying things I did not understand.

I raised him up by the hand and laughed at him. I pointed to the kid I had killed and motioned to him to fetch it. As he went, I loaded my gun again. Then, seeing what I thought was a hawk in a tree – in fact it was a parrot – I told Friday to watch me. I fired and he saw the parrot fall. He was frightened again, for he had not seen me load the gun. He thought it was a fund of death that could kill anything near or far. If I would have let him, I believe he would have worshiped me and the gun. He would not touch the gun for several days, but he spoke to it and asked it not to kill him.

We brought home the kid, and I stewed some of it and made very good broth. After I ate some, I gave some to Friday and he liked it well. It was strange to him to see me eat salt on it. He would never eat his meat with salt. The next day I roasted a leg of the kid by hanging it by a string over the fire and turning the meat often. Friday admired this very much and liked the meat so well

IF I WOULD HAVE LET HIM, I BELIEVE HE WOULD
HAVE WORSHIPED ME AND THE GUN.

I WAS VERY DELIGHTED WITH MY NEW COMPANION
AND WORKED TO TEACH HIM EVERYTHING USEFUL.

he told me he would never eat human flesh again. I was
very glad to hear this.

The next day I set him to work beating and sift-
ing some grain. After that, he watched me make bread
and bake it, and in a little time Friday could do all my
work as well as I could.

Now having two mouths to feed, I needed more
ground to plant grain. So I marked out a larger piece
and began fencing it. Friday not only worked very hard,

but very cheerfully. He let me know he thought I had more work to do because of him and that he would work harder, if I would tell him what to do.

This was the most pleasant year of all my life on the island. Friday began to talk pretty well and know the names of things. He chatted a great deal to me. I had satisfaction in the fellow himself. His simple honesty appeared to me more and more every day. I really began to love him and, on his side, I believe he loved me.

I had a mind to find out if he had any desire to go to his own country again. He had learned English so well that he could answer almost any question. I asked him if the nation he belonged to was ever victorious in battle. He smiled and said, "Yes, we always fight better." So we began the following conversation:

MASTER: "If your nation fights better, how were you taken prisoner, Friday?"

FRIDAY: "My nation beat much."

MASTER: "If your nation beat them, how were you taken?"

FRIDAY: "They many more than my nation in the place where me was. They take one, two, three,

and me. My nation beat them in other place and
take thousand."

MASTER: "Why did your people not save you
from your enemies?"

FRIDAY: "They make me go in canoe. My nation
have no canoe that time."

MASTER: "Does your nation carry away men and
eat them?"

FRIDAY: "My nation eat mans, too. Eat all up."

MASTER: "Do they come here?"

FRIDAY: "Yes, come here and other place."

MASTER: "Have you been here with them?"

FRIDAY: "Yes, I been here." [*Pointing to the
other side of the island.*]

From this I understood that Friday had been
among the savages that came on shore for the same reason he was brought for. Once when we were on the other
side of the island, he said he knew the place. He had
been there once when they ate twenty men, two women,
and a child.

I tell this because as we talked I asked if canoes
were ever lost between the island and the shore. He said

there was no danger, that no canoes were ever lost. But a little ways out to sea there was a current which went one direction in the morning and the other in the afternoon. I took these to be tides.

I asked him many questions about his country. He told me all he knew with great openness. He told me that a great way to the west lived white men with beards, like me, who had killed many men. I understood he meant the Spaniards, whose cruelties in America are widely known. He said I might get among those white men if I had a boat as large as two canoes. I began to entertain hopes of making my escape and that this savage might help me do it.

After we became more acquainted, I told him my story, how I came there and how I lived. I let him into the mystery of gunpowder and bullets and taught him how to shoot. I gave him a knife, which delighted him, and a hatchet.

I described Europe to him, especially England. I told him where I came from, how we lived, how we worshipped, how we traded with all parts of the world, and also showed him where my ship wrecked. I showed him our ship's boat, which I had tried to move, and he stood studying it a great while. At last he said, "Me see such boat like this come to my nation."

I understood that a boat such as this had come to the shore where he lived, driven by bad weather. Friday described the boat well enough for me to know it was European, adding, "We save white mens." He showed with his hands that seventeen men remained living with his people.

This put new thoughts in my head. I imagined these might be men belonging to the ship that had wrecked in sight of my island. They had saved themselves in their boat and landed on a wild shore among savages.

I asked Friday what had become of them. He said they had been living there about four years and that the savages left them alone. I asked why they did not eat them. He answered that they only ate men who were taken as prisoners in battle.

A long time after this, we were on the top of the hill. The weather being very clear, Friday looked toward the mainland in surprise and began jumping and dancing. "There see my country," he said. I saw a sense of pleasure and eagerness appear on his face and his eyes sparkled. It seemed he wished to be in his own country again. I began to worry that if he could get back to his own people he would forget all that he had said and bring them back to make a feast of me.

I wronged the poor honest creature with such thoughts and was very sorry later. But for some weeks my jealousy lasted, and I was not as kind to him as before. Every day I pumped him to learn his thoughts. But in everything he was so honest and so innocent that I could find nothing to feed my suspicions. At last I gave up suspecting him of deceit.

One day, walking on the same hill, I asked him if he wished to be in his own nation. He said, "Yes, much glad." Would you turn wild again and eat men's flesh, I asked. Shaking his head, he said, "No, no. Friday tell them live good. Eat bread. No eat man." He said he would be willing to go back if I would go with him. I said I was afraid they would eat me. "No, no," he said, "me make they no eat you." He said he would tell them how I had saved him from his enemies.

After this I had a mind to see if I could join the bearded men. I took Friday to my boat on the other side of the island, cleared it of water, brought it out, and we got in it.

I found he could handle it skillfully and make it go almost as fast as I could. "Well, now," I said to him, "shall we go to your nation?" He looked uncertain. He thought the boat was too small to go so far. I told him I had a bigger one. The next day we went to the place where I had my first boat, the one I could not get to the water. He said it was big enough, but because it had lain there 23 years and I had not taken care of it, it was split and rotten.

By this time I was fixed on the idea of going to the mainland with him. I told him we would make a boat as big as that and then he would go home in it. He looked very sad and was silent. When I asked him what was the matter, he answered, "You angry mad with Friday. What me done? Why send Friday home?" In a word, he would not think of going there without me. He ran and got one of the hatchets he used and gave it to me. "Kill Friday!" he said. "No send Friday away." I saw tears in his eyes and the great affection he had for me. I told him then I would never send him away.

Without any more delay, I went to work with Friday to find a large tree to cut down. There were enough trees on the island to build a fleet. The main thing we looked for was one so near the water we could launch it

AFTER A MONTH'S HARD LABOR, FRIDAY AND I FINISHED THE BOAT.

once it was made, and not make the mistake I made the
first time. Friday settled on a tree (he knew the kinds of
wood so much better than I) that resembled a redwood.
He was for burning out a hollow in it, but I showed him
instead how to cut it out with tools. After a month's hard
labor we finished it. It was very handsome. We cut the outside with our axes into the true shape of a boat. After this,
it took us two weeks to move it, inch by inch, on log rollers
into the water. She would have carried twenty men easily.

It amazed me to see how skillfully Friday could

manage her and paddle her along. He said he would venture in her, even in a great wind. I planned to fit her with a mast, sail, and anchor. The mast came from a straight, young cedar tree. I had pieces of old sails, of which I found two that were pretty good. With a great deal of tedious stitching, since I had no needles, I finally made a three-cornered, ugly thing, like the sail I had when I made my escape from the Moors.

I was nearly two months performing this last work. I made a small foresail, which would help when we had the wind behind us. I made a rudder to steer with, which cost me almost as much labor as making the boat, but I knew its usefulness.

Now I had to teach Friday navigation. He knew nothing about a sail and rudder and was amazed when he saw me work the boat back and forth in the sea and how the sail filled this way and that as we changed course. However, with a little practice, I made all these things familiar to him. He became an expert sailor, except that he could never understand a compass.

I was now in my twenty-seventh year of captivity in this place. The last three years, when I had Friday with me, ought to be left out of the count because my life was

NOW I HAD TO TEACH FRIDAY NAVIGATION.

quite a bit different than in the rest of the time. I kept the anniversary of my landing with the same thankfulness to God as I had at the first. I had great hopes that I would not be another year in this place, but I went on with my digging and planting as usual.

In the meantime, the rainy season came on. We stowed our vessel in the creek in a dock Friday dug and covered her with branches to keep rain off her. Thus we waited for the months of November and December, when I planned to make my adventure.

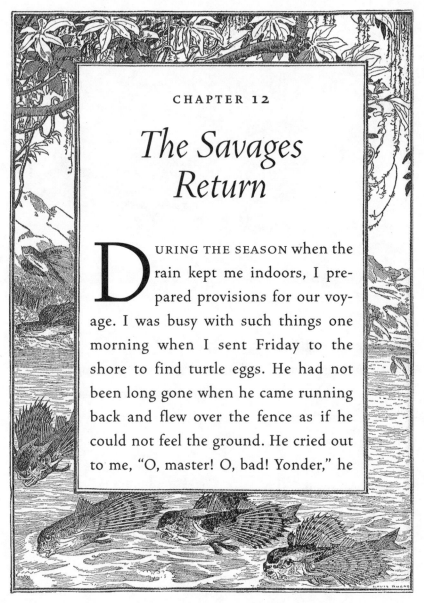

CHAPTER 12

The Savages Return

URING THE SEASON when the rain kept me indoors, I prepared provisions for our voyage. I was busy with such things one morning when I sent Friday to the shore to find turtle eggs. He had not been long gone when he came running back and flew over the fence as if he could not feel the ground. He cried out to me, "O, master! O, bad! Yonder," he said, "one, two, three canoe!"

"Friday," I said, "Do not be frightened." However, I saw the fellow was terribly scared. He thought the savages had come to look for him and eat him. He trembled so I hardly knew what to do to comfort him. I told him I was in as much danger as he was and that we must fight. "Can you fight, Friday?" I asked. " Me shoot," he said, "but there many great number."

"No matter," I said. "Our guns will frighten the ones we do not kill." I asked him if he would stand by me and do just as I told him. He said, "Me die when you say die, master." I made him take two fowling pieces, loaded with large shot, and I took four muskets loaded with five bullets each. I took two pistols and hung my naked sword at my side. Friday had his hatchet.

Thus prepared, I took my spyglass up the hill to see what I could see. I saw 21 savages, three prisoners, and three canoes. Their business seemed to be to have a banquet of human bodies, nothing more than was usual among them.

They had landed, not where they came when Friday made his escape, but nearer to my creek next to a thick woods. Despising the business they came on, I was

I PUT DOWN ONE MUSKET AND TOOK AIM WITH THE OTHER.

filled with such anger that I told Friday I intended to kill them all. I asked him if he would stand by me. Very cheerfully he said, as he had before, "I die when you say die."

In this fury, I divided up the weapons we had and put a small bottle of rum in my pocket. Friday took a large bag with more powder and bullets. I ordered him to stay close beside me and not to shoot or speak or do anything until I told him. We traveled a long way around to get within range of them without being discovered.

I entered the woods with all possible wariness

and silence. Friday followed close at my heels. We marched until only one corner of the woods lay between them and us. Here I pointed out a great tree to Friday and told him to go to it and bring me word of what he could see. He came back immediately and said the savages could be plainly seen around their fire eating one of the prisoners. Another prisoner, who they would kill next, lay bound upon the sand a little ways away. This fired my soul, for he told me this prisoner was one of the bearded men. I was filled with horror and went to the tree. I saw plainly in my spyglass a white man on the beach, with his hands and feet tied. He was a European and had clothes on.

There was a little thicket 50 yards nearer them than the place I was. Going behind some bushes, I reached it unseen and got behind another tree. I had not a moment to lose. Nineteen of the wretches sat on the ground, all huddled together, and had just sent the other two to butcher the poor European. As they stooped to untie the vines at his feet, I said to Friday, "Do exactly what you see me do." I put down one musket and a fowling piece and took aim with the other musket. I fired and at the same moment Friday fired also.

Friday's aim was so much better than mine that on the first shot he killed two and wounded three. I killed one and wounded two. The savages who were not hurt jumped to their feet, but did not know which way to run or from which direction their destruction came. I threw down the musket and picked up the fowling piece. Friday did the same. I fired again into the amazed savages and so did Friday. Only two dropped, but so many were wounded they ran about yelling and screaming, like mad creatures, most of them all bloody. Soon three more fell down, though not dead.

"Now, Friday," I said, "follow me." I picked up the other musket, which was still loaded, and rushed out of the woods. Friday, with a great deal of courage, came close behind me. As soon as they saw me, I shouted as loud as I could and told Friday to shout as well. I ran as fast as I could to the victim. His two butchers left him and fled to a canoe. Three of the rest ran the same way. Friday ran another forty yards nearer to them to shoot and when he fired I thought he killed them all, but he only killed two.

While Friday fired, I took my knife and cut the bonds from the poor victim. I lifted him up and asked him in Portuguese who he was. He answered, faintly, that he was Spanish. I took the bottle out of my pocket and gave him a drink. He made signs that he was in my debt for saving him. I said, with as much Spanish as I knew, "We will talk later. We must fight now." He took a pistol and sword thankfully and flew upon his murderers like fury, cutting two of them to pieces.

The poor creatures were frightened by the noise of our guns, and they fell down in fear. They did not try to escape. I sent Friday back to the tree we had first fired from to fetch our weapons. He did it with swiftness. Then I sat down to reload. Meanwhile, the bold Spaniard was in a fierce fight with a strong savage who was about to kill him with a great wooden sword. The Spaniard, who was weak, was thrown on the ground. As the savage tried to wrestle my sword from the Spaniard's hand, the Spaniard pulled the pistol from his belt and shot, killing the savage on the spot.

Friday chased the wretches with his hatchet and killed three who were wounded. The Spaniard took a fowling piece and wounded two who were running into the woods. Friday pursued them there and killed one, but the other, who was too nimble, reached the shore and swam out to the canoe. The four now in the canoe, two of whom were wounded, paddled hard to get out of gunshot.

Friday made two or three shots at them, but did not hit any. I was very anxious about their escape, lest they bring back two or three hundred more upon us. So I decided to pursue them by sea. Jumping in one of their canoes, I was surprised to find another poor creature there bound hand and foot for slaughter and almost dead with fear. He had not been able to look over the side of the boat and had been tied tightly so long there was little life left in him.

I immediately cut the twisted vines that bound him. He could not speak or stand, but only groaned pitifully. He seemed to believe he was about to be killed. Friday came up and I asked him to tell the prisoner he was safe. When Friday looked in his face it would have moved anyone to tears to see how he kissed him, hugged him, cried, laughed, hollered, sang, danced, and jumped like a crazy creature. It was a while before he could speak to me. When he calmed himself, he told me this was his father.

It is not easy for me to put in words how moved I was by how affection worked in this poor savage at the sight of his father and his being delivered from death. He

FRIDAY LOOKED INTO THE PRISONER'S FACE AND REALIZED
WITH MUCH JOY THAT IT WAS HIS FATHER.

went in the boat and held his father's head next to him and rubbed his numbed arms and ankles. This put an end to our pursuit of the canoe, which was almost out of sight.

Friday was so busy with his father that I did not have the heart to call him. But after a while I asked him if he had any bread to give his father. He shook his head and said, "None, ugly dog eat all up." He meant himself. So I gave him some bread and raisins I carried in a little pouch. He no sooner gave these to his father than he ran away from the boat (he was the swiftest fellow on foot that I ever saw) and was out of sight in an instant. In a quarter of an hour I saw him coming back, though not as fast, because he had something in his hand.

He had been home for an earthen jug to bring his father fresh water. He also brought more cakes of bread. After his father drank, I asked Friday to give some water to the Spaniard, who was as much in want of it. The Spaniard, who sat in the shade of a tree, took bread and raisins, too. He looked at me thankfully. He tried to stand, but he was so weak and his ankles were swelled so painfully from the vines that he could not.

I had Friday carry the Spaniard down to the boat

where his father was. He launched the boat off and paddled it along the shore toward home faster than I could walk.

As soon as I had given my weak, rescued prisoners shelter and beds of rice straw, I began to think of how to provide for them. I ordered Friday to kill a yearling goat and stew it with rice and barley. After we ate, I ordered Friday to fetch our muskets and other weapons from the place of battle. The next day, I ordered him to bury the bodies of the savages and the horrible remains of their feast. He performed this so well that I hardly knew the place the next time I came to it.

I entered into a conversation with my new subjects, with Friday acting as interpreter, for the Spaniard spoke the language of the savages pretty well. I had Friday ask his father if he thought the escaping savages would return with more men than we could resist. His opinion was that they were so frightened by the manner of the attack, the noise and the fire, that they would tell their people the others had been killed by thunder and lightning, not by men. They did not think men could kill at a distance. He was right. Years later, I learned that the four men had survived. They told their people the island was enchanted and that whoever went there would be destroyed by fire from the gods.

But I did not know this then and always kept up my guard. In time, however, since no canoes appeared, I returned to my former thoughts of voyaging to the mainland. But these thoughts cooled when I had a serious talk with the Spaniard. The sixteen of his countrymen were indeed at peace with the savages, but lacked so many necessities that they were barely alive. Their ship had been bound from Rio de la Plata to Havana, carrying chiefly hides and silver. They were to bring back European goods. Five of their men drowned in the wreck and those that escaped almost starved before they arrived on the cannibal coast. They still expected to be eaten every minute.

He told me they often talked of escape, but because they had no vessel and no tools to make one, their talks always ended in despair. I asked him if he thought they would consider a plan of escape from me.

He answered that they were so miserable they would not be unkind to any man who offered to help them. He offered to go to his men with Friday's father and bring them to me with their solemn vow that they accepted me as their commander. He said he would be the first to swear to me and said his men were so out of hope he was sure they would agree, too.

With these assurances, I decided to try to relieve them, if possible, and to send the old savage and the Spaniard to the mainland to get them. The Spaniard advised that we delay half a year in order to grow more food. My stock of grain would not be enough for the four of us as well as all his countrymen to make a voyage to the American colonies.

His advice was so good that all four of us fell to digging and in a month we planted 22 bushels of barley and sixteen of rice.

During the six months we waited for our crop, we went freely all over the island, no longer fearing the savages. I found several trees fit for our shipbuilding, which I set Friday and his father to cutting down.

At the same time, I tried to increase my flock of tame goats. By hunting every day, we added about twenty kids. I also had enough raisins dried to have filled, I believe, 80 barrels.

Our crop being enough to meet our needs and safely stored in baskets, I gave the Spaniard permission to go to the mainland. He and Friday's father left in one of the canoes that they came in as prisoners. I gave each of them a musket, about eight rounds of ammunition, and provisions of bread and grapes sufficient for many days. We agreed on a signal they would hang out on their return, so that I would know them before they came ashore. I waited for them eight days when a strange accident happened.

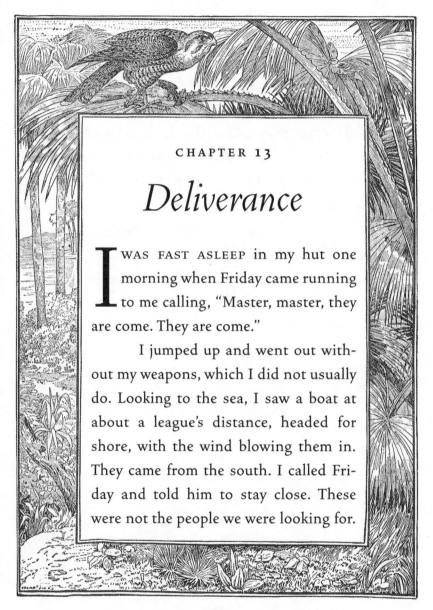

CHAPTER 13

Deliverance

I WAS FAST ASLEEP in my hut one morning when Friday came running to me calling, "Master, master, they are come. They are come."

I jumped up and went out without my weapons, which I did not usually do. Looking to the sea, I saw a boat at about a league's distance, headed for shore, with the wind blowing them in. They came from the south. I called Friday and told him to stay close. These were not the people we were looking for.

And we did not know yet whether they were friends or enemies.

I went to fetch my spyglass and climbed to the top of the hill to take my view without being seen. I had scarcely set foot there when I discovered a ship lying at anchor toward the south about a league-and-a-half offshore. It appeared to be an English ship.

I felt joy at seeing a ship from my own country, but I also had some doubts that made me keep up my guard. I did not know what business an English ship had in a part of the world where the English rarely came. It was possible they were really thieves and murderers. No one should ignore such hints of danger.

Soon the longboat landed on the beach, about a half a mile from me. I was certain they were Englishmen. There were eleven in all, three of whom were unarmed and bound. They were taken out of the boat as prisoners. The three made pleading gestures and lifted up their hands in despair.

Friday said to me, "O master! You see English mans eat prisoner just like savage mans." "No, no," I said. "I am afraid they will murder them, but they will not eat them."

I had no idea what the matter really was. But I stood trembling, expecting at every moment that the three prisoners would be killed. Once I saw one of the villains lift his sword as if he meant to strike one of the poor men.

I wished heartily now for my Spaniard and the savage that went with him. After I had watched the insulting treatment of the three men by the seamen, I saw the seamen scatter to look around the shore and the three other men sit down on the ground sadly. This made me think of how I felt when I first came on shore and gave myself up for lost. Just as I knew not how I might be saved, so these men knew nothing of how near deliverance was to them.

It was high tide when they came ashore and while they rambled the tide went out, leaving their longboat aground. Two men who had stayed with it fell asleep. One awoke and called the rest to try to launch the boat. But the boat was very heavy and the sand very soft, almost like quicksand. I heard one of them call to another, "Let her alone, Jack. She'll float with the next tide." This proved they were English. They gave up trying and strolled away again.

Meanwhile, I readied myself for battle. I was more careful, because I knew I had another kind of enemy than before. I ordered Friday, who was an excellent marksman now, to load himself with weapons. I took two fowling pieces and gave him three muskets. My appearance was indeed very fierce looking. I had my goatskin coat on, my large cap, a sword at my side, two pistols in my belt, and a gun on each shoulder.

About two o'clock, in the heat of the day, I found they had all straggled into the woods and laid down to sleep. The three poor men, too worried to sleep, sat down in the shade of a tree and seemed to be out of sight of the rest.

I decided to show myself to them. I marched as near as I could to them without being seen, with Friday a good distance behind me, and called to them in Spanish, "Who are you, gentlemen?"

They jumped up at the sound and were startled to see me. They made no answer and seemed about to run away. So I spoke to them in English. "Gentlemen, do not be surprised at me. You may have a friend you did not expect."

"He must be sent from heaven then," said one of them, as he pulled off his hat.

"GENTLEMEN, DO NOT BE SURPRISED AT ME.
YOU MAY HAVE A FRIEND YOU DID NOT EXPECT."

"All help is from heaven," said I. "What is your
distress? When you landed, I saw one of them raise his
sword to kill you."

"Our story is too long to tell while murderers are so near," he answered. "In short, sir, I was the captain of that ship. My men mutinied against me and have set us ashore on this deserted place. These men with me are my mate and a passenger. We expected to perish, believing the island to be uninhabited."

"Where have your enemies gone?" I said.

"There, sir," he said, pointing to a thicket of trees. "I fear they may have seen us or heard you speak. If they have, I am sure they will kill us all."

I said, "Leave the rest to me. I see they are all asleep. It would be easy to kill them. Or shall we take them prisoner?"

He told me there were two men among them who it would not be safe to show mercy to, but if they were bound, he believed the others would return to their duty.

I said I was willing to try to save him if he would agree to two things. "First, while you stay with me you will be governed by my orders. Second, if the ship is recovered, you will give me and my man free passage to England." He gave me promises and said he would always acknowledge that he owed his life to me.

"Well, then," I said, "Here are three muskets."

He said he did not want to kill them if he could help it. But if the two villains escaped, they might reach the ship and bring the rest of the mutineers to destroy us.

As we were talking, we heard some of them awaken and saw two on their feet. Seeing that a chance to capture them might slip away, the captain and his two men went toward them. A seamen saw them coming and called out to the rest, but it was too late. As he cried out, the captain's two men fired (the captain wisely saved his shot). They had aimed so well at the villains that one was killed on the spot. The other was wounded, but stood up. The captain knocked him down with the stock of his musket so that he never spoke again. The three other seamen, as I came up, saw it was useless to resist and begged for mercy. The captain said he would spare their lives if they would swear to be faithful to him in recovering the ship and sailing her back to Jamaica. They swore, and he believed them and spared their lives. I was not against it, but I ordered him to keep them bound, hand and foot, while they were on the island.

Meanwhile, I sent Friday and the captain's mate to the boat to take away her sail and oars. By and by, three stragglers appeared. They had come back upon hearing guns fired. Seeing that their captain, once their prisoner, was now their conqueror, they surrendered and were also tied up. Our victory was complete.

I now told the captain my whole history, which he listened to with amazement. It seemed to him that I had been preserved there to save his life. Tears ran down his face. After this, I brought him and his men to my dwelling, where I refreshed them with food and showed them all the things I had made during my long, long stay in that place.

At present, our business was to recover the ship. The captain was at a loss for how to do it. There were still 26 men on board, who would fight desperately. They knew that if they were overpowered they would be brought to the gallows as soon as they came to England or any of the colonies.

I mused for some time over what he said and found a logical conclusion: to draw the men on board into a trap. It occurred to me that in a little while the men on board would wonder what became of their comrades and come ashore to look for them.

The first thing we had to do was stave the longboat so she could not float. We carried away all the supplies in her and knocked a great hole in her bottom, so that if they mastered us, they yet could not have the boat. Indeed, I did not think we could recover the ship, but if it left without the boat, I was certain we could repair her and sail to our friends, the Spaniards.

While we were making the hole, we heard the ship fire a gun and saw her raise a flag, signaling the boat to return. But no boat stirred, so they fired several more times. At last, they hoisted another boat out and rowed toward shore. With the help of my spyglass, I saw ten men in her, all armed. We had a full view of them as they came, even their faces.

Three of them, the captain said, were honest fellows who were forced into the conspiracy. But the boatswain, their chief officer, and the rest were as outrageous and desperate as any of the crew could be. I smiled at him and told him we were past fear. Anything that might happen to us in our present state, death or life, would be deliverance for us. Depend on it, I said, every man who came ashore would be in our hands.

I spoke cheerfully and it encouraged him. Meanwhile, I sent Friday with the prisoners to our cave, where there was no danger of them being heard. They were left bound, but with food and candles, and promised that if they tried to escape they would be put to death. They promised to bear their confinement patiently.

Two of the prisoners we kept with us, on the captain's recommendation, so now we were seven armed men. I had no doubt we could deal well enough with the ten that were coming.

When they came to the place where the longboat was, they ran their boat onto the beach and then hauled it out of the water. They all ran to the other boat, and it was easy to see how surprised they were to find her empty and with a hole in her bottom. Then they shouted two or three times with all their might. When there was no answer, they came together in a circle and let go a volley of their pistols, which made the woods ring with echoes. They were so astonished at all of this that they launched their boat to return to the ship to let their friends know the longboat was staved.

Soon after they set off, they turned around again. It seems they decided to leave three men in the boat and send the rest up into the country looking for their fellows. This disappointed us, for seizing those seven men would do us no good if the boat escaped back to the ship.

The ship would then surely set sail, and the chance of recovering it would be lost. However, we had no remedy but to wait and see what might happen.

The seven men came ashore and the three others anchored a good distance out and waited. It was impossible to come at them. Those on shore kept close together and marched toward the little hill where my dwelling was. We could see them plainly, but they could not perceive us. Along the way they shouted and called out, until they tired and sat under a tree to rest.

We waited a long time, very impatiently. After a discussion, they stood up and began marching to the sea. It seems they feared danger and decided to give up their companions as lost. When I saw they were giving up their search, I thought of a plan to fetch them back again.

I ordered Friday and the captain's mate to go about a half a mile to the west, to the place where the savages landed, and holler as loud as they could. As soon as they heard the seamen answer them, they should return to us again, keeping out of sight and always answering a holler, so as to draw the seamen as far into the woods as possible.

The seamen were just climbing into their boat when they heard Friday and the mate call. Answering, they ran along the shore to the west. Presently they were stopped by the creek, which they could not get over. They called for their boat, as indeed, I expected.

Once they got over, they fastened the boat to a stump and left two men with her. This is what I wished for. Leaving Friday and the mate to their business, I took the rest and crossed the creek, surprising the two men. These were two who were not willing in the mutiny. They were easily persuaded to join us.

In the meantime, Friday and the mate managed so well that by hollering and answering they drew the seamen from hill to hill, from one wood to another, until they were heartily tired and could not reach the boat again before dark. Indeed, Friday and the mate were very tired by the time they came back to us.

We had nothing to do but watch for them in the dark and fall on them. It was several hours before they reached their boat. We could hear the first one call to those behind to hurry along and hear them complain of how lame and weary they were. This was welcome news to us.

They were greatly confused when they found their boat left aground in the creek by the ebb of the tide and their two men gone. We heard them tell one another they were on an enchanted island, where inhabitants would murder them or else devils would carry them away. By what little light there was, we saw them sit by their boat or walk about in despair.

I drew my ambush nearer. I ordered Friday and the captain to creep on their hands and knees as close as they possibly could without being seen. They had not long been near when the boatswain, the ringleader of the mutiny, now more dejected than the rest, came walking towards them with two others. The captain was so eager to have the rogue in his power that he could hardly wait for him to come closer. He and Friday jumped to their feet and fired.

The boatswain was killed on the spot and the man next to him fell down, shot in the body. He died an hour later. The third ran for it. At the noise of the guns, I advanced with my army. In the dark, they could not see how many we were. I made the man next to me, who knew their names, call out to them to surrender. "Tom Smith, throw down your arms and yield," he said, "or you are all dead in the next minute."

"Surrender to whom?" one answered.

The captain then called out, "Lay down your arms while you have your lives and trust in the governor's mercy." (They called me governor.) They knew his voice and laid down their guns. I ordered them bound, but kept myself and Friday out of sight.

Our next work was to repair the boat and seize the ship. I told the captain my plan for taking the ship, which he liked well, and we resolved to attempt it in the morning. First, we divided the prisoners. Some of the worst, with their hands tied, were sent with Friday to the cave. The captain asked the rest if they would join him to retake the ship to earn a pardon for their mutiny. They fell on their knees before him and promised to be faithful to him to their last drop of blood. Our strength for the attack was now twelve men. Friday and I would stay to guard the five prisoners in the cave.

The captain now fixed the hole in the longboat and made his passenger its leader, with four men. The captain, his mate, and five others went in the other boat. They came up to the ship about midnight. As they came near, they hailed the ship and told those on board that they had brought the men and boat back. They kept up chatting as they came along the ship's side.

The captain and his mate entered first, and immediately knocked down a mate and the carpenter with the butt-ends of their muskets. Followed by their men, they captured all on the deck of the ship and fastened the hatches, to keep those below trapped. When all was safe on deck, the mate and three men broke into the cabin where the rebel captain was. He fired on the mate and wounded him in the arm, but the mate rushed on and shot the rebel through the head. At that, the rest surrendered and no more lives were lost.

The captain ordered seven guns fired, which was our signal for success. It was near two o'clock in the morning. I was so tired I laid down and slept. Presently, I heard a man calling me governor. It was the captain. He embraced me and, pointing to the ship, said, "My friend, there is your ship. She is yours, and so are we." They anchored her at the mouth of the creek.

I saw deliverance put into my hands, a ship ready to carry me wherever I pleased. For some time, I was not able to say a word. I held onto him, otherwise I would have fallen to the ground. There was such joy in me that I broke out in tears.

We rejoiced together. I told him I looked upon him as a man sent from heaven to save me, and that events had been a chain of wonders. I thanked God for the miracle.

The captain brought me presents from the things the wretches had not plundered: six bottles of wine, two pounds of tobacco, twelve pieces of the ship's beef and pork, biscuits, a box of sugar, a box of flour, and a bag of lemons. The most useful things he brought were a pair of shoes, a hat, clean new shirts, and a very good suit of clothes. Never was anything in the world so unpleasant and awkward to me as wearing these clothes for the first time.

After this ceremony, we began to talk about what to do with our prisoners. We might dare to take them with us, except for the two who were **incorrigible**. The captain said they were such rogues they must be carried away in irons and hanged at the first English colony he came to. I told him we should leave them on the island.

INCORRIGIBLE
Someone who refuses to be corrected or reformed.

I had the men brought before me, as governor, and told them that I knew of their villainous behavior to the captain. I let them know they could see the reward their new captain had received for his villainy, for they could see him hanging from a yard arm of the ship. When I said I did not know why I should not hang them as pirates too, they humbly begged for mercy from me.

I said I was inclined to give them their liberty on the island. They seemed thankful and said they would rather stay there than be carried to the gallows in England. I was as good as my word and set them free, telling them I would give them directions of how to live.

I told them my whole history and showed them my fort, the way I made bread, planted corn, and cured grapes, how I managed goats, and how to make cheese. I also told them the story of the Spaniards whom I expected to return, for whom I left a letter, and made them promise to treat the Spaniards as themselves. I left them five muskets, gunpowder, and garden seeds.

The next day I went on board the ship. By way of relics, I took with me my goatskin cap, my umbrella, and my parrot. I also took the money I have mentioned. I left the island on the 19th of December, 1686, after having been on it 28 years, two months and 19 days. I was delivered from this captivity on the anniversary of the day that I made my escape from the Moors. I arrived in England in June, having been gone 35 years.

MY NEPHEW ENGAGED ME TO GO WITH HIM
AS A TRADER TO THE EAST INDIES.

I was a perfect stranger to all the world, as if I had never been known there. I went to Yorkshire and found my father and mother and all my family dead, except two nephews, and that I had long ago been given up for dead. Friday accompanied me on all these ramblings and proved a faithful servant on all occasions.

I inquired of my old friend in Lisbon, the sea captain who first took me to Brazil, to learn of my partner and plantation. He knew that my partner had grown rich on his part of it, and that since we were both alive, there would be no question of my part being restored to me. In a few months I received a letter from my partner, who congratulated me on being alive and settled on me £5,000 of money and hundreds of chests of sugar and rolls of tobacco. I was in a condition of wealth I could scarcely understand.

I took my two nephews into my care. The eldest I raised as a gentleman and gave him an estate. The other, a sensible bold fellow, I made the captain of a ship. He engaged me to go with him as a trader to the East Indies in the year 1694. In this voyage, I visited my island and saw the colony begun there by the Spaniards. I heard the story of their lives and how at last they had used violence against the villains I left there. I found five women and twenty children on the island. I stayed there about twenty days and left them supplies of all necessary things. I urged them not to leave and, despite attacks by the Indians, they live there still.

Daniel Defoe

1 6 6 0 - 1 7 3 1

DANIEL DEFOE was born in London, England. His father was a candle merchant and butcher. His mother died when he was about ten. His family were Presbyterians, who were called Puritans or

Dissenters then because they disagreed with the rules of the Church of England. Defoe studied at a Dissenter academy, where science, modern languages, and English composition were stressed.

He was raised to be plain and sensible, but he sometimes liked to be showy and reckless. He joined a rebellion against King James II and was lucky to escape being executed after the rebel army was crushed.

Although he had intended to be a minister, he instead took up trading in hosiery, wine, and tobacco and traveled through Europe and Britain. At age 32, he went bankrupt, partly because he liked risky, high-stakes deals. He began manufacturing bricks and tiles and tried to pay back his debts. After his brick factory failed, people to whom he owed money hounded him for the rest of his life.

Though he never gave up making business deals, Defoe went on to become England's first true political reporter. Crafty, persuasive, and hardworking, he wrote at least 566 separate works. He was a spy for King William III and secretly wrote essays defending him. Publicly, he said he was liberal. But while Queen Anne reigned, he wrote secretly for the conservatives. When the queen died, he became a double agent and revealed the conservatives' plans to the government. In his own day, many people thought he was a rascal.

Defoe once published an essay, without his name on it, in which he pretended to demand that Dissenters like him be crucified. When his authorship was uncovered, he was pilloried (forced to stand at a post with his neck and hands locked between two planks) for three days. People usually threw rocks and rotten vegetables at those being pilloried, but Defoe won the crowd over. He handed out a poem that mocked his judges and struck a defiant pose. So, instead, people threw flowers.

The Review, a paper he produced alone, came out three times a week for nine years. He wrote on every subject, especially economics, and took ideas he liked from wherever he found them. A firm Puritan, he often told his readers they should rely on their own efforts and be responsible for their actions.

He wrote *Robinson Crusoe*, his most famous book, when he was 59. Many think of it as the first English novel. It was so well-loved that people often stated in their will who should inherit their copy.

Defoe died at age 71 in a London boarding house, where he was hiding from people to whom he owed money.